Short Happy Stories

by Evan Pellervo

Paperback ISBN 979-8-9895787-0-2
eBook ISBN 979-8-9895787-1-9

Library of Congress Control Number: 2024902708

Published by Manaatti Books

Pacific Grove, California

And then he's gone and she's alone with the statue of Seabiscuit and two swaying palm trees and a fluttering American flag. Well, she isn't *actually* alone, there are quite a few other people around—some are hurrying with a clear destination in mind, some are ambling along with apparent aimlessness, some are discussing horses and jockeys with gravity, some are laughing, some are standing still and not making a sound and staring at their racing forms—but she is barely aware of their existence. For her, all of life has been compressed into one question: *How do I win?*

Contents

Before The Printing Press

It really is almost over now, the trees seem to be saying, sadly. In many places the ground can no longer be seen, due to orange and yellow and purple and red and brown leaves, which release sharp sounds when stepped on. The sun has been spending less and less of its time in visible sky. The trees are correct: fall has been falling for quite a while now, and it is now quite close to its terminus.

We villagers dread the winter and always have. The winter is so dreadful because once the snow begins to stick it doesn't go away for months and months, and it builds and builds and transfigures—simplifies—reality into a monolithic monotony, and exiting our little village becomes almost an impossibility, and in the nights we sit around and listen to the creaking of our small structures, and for the first few nights this is all alright because we have warm hearths and hot tea, but then the nights become—and stay—very, very, very boring.

It's still early when I look up from the trough I'm filling and see a friend approaching. He tells me he just saw some squirrels scampering on some almost bare branches, and I tell him I see scampering squirrels all the time, there is nothing at all unusual about squirrels scampering. But when he saw the scampering squirrels just now, he tells me, an idea presented itself to him.

Can you tell me what idea presented itself to you?

The dreaded dreadful winter is yet again—and so soon!—almost here, and maybe this year we should try something new. Maybe this year we should follow the example of the squirrels, who, every year, gather *everything* that will be useful after the snow arrives before the snow arrives; though we villagers have always gathered *many* useful things before the snow arrives, there may be other things out there that could, just possibly…

Since we are exceedingly aware of the falling fall—we must take action while we still can!—we abandon our previous plans for the day and set out immediately.

Horses bear us out of our little village and along a path with almost bare trees on both sides. In this cold air the air that comes out of the horses' noses is visible, briefly, and the air that comes out of our noses is also visible, briefly. "Breath" would probably be a better word to use. Our breaths are briefly visible. The sky is the way that allows us to look at the sun without hurting our eyes.

When the old, old wall of the old, old, old town makes itself visible, at the base of the big hill in the distance, we begin to discuss how to approach our task.

After a not very long discussion, we agree that the main thing to do is try to be friendly. Because what's the worst that can happen if we are friendly?

Our timing turns out to be good: as we ride into town a bell rings twelve times, and the first tavern we look into contains quite a few people eating and drinking. We both order mead, in order to make the proprietor and the patrons think mead is our reason for being there. Then we begin to circulate. The first two people we try to talk with are not receptive; since their lack of interest in us is definite, we don't even ask those first two people our important question. The third person, though, is quite eager to engage with us—several empty vessels in front of him suggest that spirits have lifted his spirit, even though it's barely noon—and he even encourages us to sit close to him. We sit close to him, and quickly infer, from the confusing movements of his hands and the lack of articulation in his speech, drunkenness. Though we would rather not talk at length with a lush, winter is coming and we are desperate; so we ask him if he could tell us a story.

You want a story? he says, and we say, nodding, Yes.

He doesn't say anything for one... two... three... four... five... six... sev—And suddenly he launches into a story, and suddenly the movements of his hands are deliberate and effective, and his words are distinct; and, best of all, his story turns out to be really, really good. The ending is very surprising! Though he claims his story is completely true, we don't quite believe him—some really incredible things happen in his story!—but we don't actually care if his story is true or not. The only thing we want a story to be is really, really good.

Over the next several hours we talk with quite a few other people, both in the tavern and elsewhere in town, and by the time we ride our horses out of town we have collected seven solid stories. Back in our little village we tell the others what we have done and encourage them to do the same before the snow arrives. The snow arrives one week later, and in the nights in our snow-enveloped structures we share the stories we collected. Almost everyone in our little village went over to the old, old, old town at least once to collect stories, so our little village now has almost one hundred stories at its disposal.

In this snow world the moon makes everything except the glowing windows—which from a distance look like pumpkins, and behind which imaginations are at work—silver. The story entering our consciousness transfigures our familiar walls into palaces and prisons, into seas and sands, into distant paradises. Or, no, not distant: this place—this warm, enveloped-by-snow place—is now paradise.

4

When we have all heard all of the stories we collected before the snow's arrival, we begin to invent our own stories—how had we never thought of that before?—and before we know it the leaves are back on the trees, who seem to be saying, with calm relief, I'm glad that's over.

A Cloud

A single small cloud is in the sky, as though the world has a single small thought. Maybe this thought of the world is unrelated to what is happening below, to the people going this way and that way and other ways too, sometimes accomplishing things they want to accomplish and sometimes not accomplishing things they want to accomplish, some of them convinced of meaning and some of them wondering if any of this has any point. Or maybe this thought of the world—whatever it is—is not unrelated to what is happening below. Or maybe the world does not have a single small thought. How is anyone to ever know? In any case, that single small cloud is very nice to look at, as it slowly, so slowly, floats along.

Little Adjustments

As she moves between bricks and spring leaves, toward a resolute wooden door, her envy grows. In addition to the incredible career—the kind of career she wishes she had—he has this incredible property. On the edge of a sparkling lake. She seldom accepts jobs this far out of the city, but knew she would accept this one as soon as the caller gave his name, because she loves his work. But now she is wondering if it was a mistake to drive out here. Because… Because he has this wonderful brick path, these wonderful spring leaves, this wonderful resolute door, that wonderful sparkling lake—and what does she have? She doesn't have the accomplishments she'd hoped to have by now, in her thirties, she can tell you that. What she *does* have is her kit—which, after years, feels more like an extension of her left hand than something her left hand is merely holding. She pushes the doorbell with her right index finger.

"Please excuse the mess," says the oldish man—whom she of course recognizes—as he leads her through the house, which is indisputably a mess, with opened and unopened boxes scattered around. *Please excuse the mess.*

What a jerk. He can't possibly care if she does or does not excuse the mess, she feels certain of that. It's just one of those things people say to fill empty space. Or to pretend to be considerate. But what's wrong with that? Nothing. Nothing at all. She is self-aware enough to know that she's only irritated because she's jealous of his success. She is also self-aware enough to know that even though she loves his work, she won't say anything about it.

The piano turns out to be a mahogany Model M, in the midcentury modern style. The piano is next to big windows—*sun damage*, she thinks, *is definitely a possibility*—so a player can look at the pale blue lake and the crisp mountains beyond the pale blue lake.

"Do you need anything? Would you like some water?"

She tells him she has everything she needs.

With what she suspects is great intentionality, he creates a smile that is clearly meant to be friendly, and this annoys her even though she should maybe appreciate it more than a smile that is automatically, naturally friendly, since more effort is involved. "Then I'll leave you to it," he says. Then he points toward another part of the house. "I'll be in the study at the end of that hallway there."

As he walks away she opens her kit and takes out the tuning wrench. As she listens to the middle C she watches a small motorboat draw a white line on the pale blue lake. The white line is almost perfectly perpendicular to the windowsill, and she imagines the white line extending all the way to the other side of the lake and onto the mountains and into the sky. But of course that won't happen, because the drawing tool is a motorboat.

She begins to make adjustments, to make the strings exactly the way they should be. The world has a surfeit of ambiguities, a surfeit of questions that are too difficult to answer with certainty, but there *is* an agreed-upon way to properly tune a piano, which is a fact she finds comforting.

Having spent so much time tuning pianos over the last few years, she is able to listen to the notes she plays and make the necessary adjustments while another part of her mind remembers the newspaper article, approximately five years ago, informing her that the owner of the piano she is now tuning would be in town for a one-week residency at an esteemed jazz club. Immediately she knew she wanted to attend one of his shows, as she had loved several of his quintet's albums. She even felt as though her own piano playing had been positively influenced by things she had learned from his piano playing.

A few days later she was in the audience with a friend—whom, she now realizes, she hasn't seen in quite some time—and the show was fantastic. It was constantly obvious that all five players were really *listening* to each other; they freewheelingly constructed tremendously compelling, tremendously *inventive* connections. Tremendous! What a tremendous show!

When the tremendous show was over she and her friend—*you really should*, she thinks as she turns the tuning wrench, *catch up with him one of these days; it has been way too long*—were tremendously invigorated and walked for a not insignificant period of time through fog-filled streets, where streetlamps were producing nebulous orange spheres. They were discussing, in great detail, the music they had just heard, and their discussion became their whole world. To them it was an interesting and pleasant world. The fog made it hard to see things, which helped push everyday reality and its corresponding concerns beyond concern. Beyond consideration, even. Almost beyond existence.

As they approached the next nebulous orange sphere a dark figure within the sphere gradually gained definition, transforming from a blob into a man in a dark gray suit, sitting on the sidewalk, leaning against the streetlamp. His body did not appear to be moving at all, and he was hunched over in such a way that he could just as easily be dead as alive. Both walkers, suspecting that the former possibility was the truth, moved close to the suited man. Exactly one moment after they were close enough to determine that he was still breathing, he opened his eyes and leapt to his feet. If they hadn't instinctively leapt back when he leapt up, he probably would have bumped into them.

Standing there with his arms at his sides, the suited man started to yell. It was scary. He kept yelling. It was scary. Instead of continuing on their way, though, they listened to the suited man—maybe because they had so recently been in the presence of those musicians who listened to each other so well. Whatever the reason, they listened to the yelling of the suited man—whose suit was surprisingly nice and clean, whose hair was actually quite well combed, whose face was smooth—and nothing was comprehensible. They realized that even though he was looking in their direction as he yelled, he wasn't actually looking *at* them. They realized that he wasn't trying to communicate with them at all. He was just yelling at himself. Or maybe at God. Or maybe at nothing.

They resumed their walk, leaving the suited man where he stood, but things weren't the same as before. Their interesting and pleasant world had been shattered by the suited man. After listening to the suited man it seemed as though reality was one big failure, as though there were too many problems for any happiness to be justified and sane. But then she remembered an amazing thing the pianist had done, and, with some hesitance, mentioned the amazing thing to her friend, who then shared a thought on a semi-related thing the drummer had done—and just like that, so quickly, their interesting and pleasant world was glued back together.

The motorboat is no longer visible. The lake and the mountains and the sky are still visible, but they all look at least slightly different from how they looked before. Because of changing light.

Yes, she wishes she could have achieved a career comparable to this guy's, wishes she could live in a place like this. She really *does* envy him. But... Whatever. Before she leaves, she decides, she'll tell him that she has loved his music for years. Maybe she'll even tell him that once, in the middle of a foggy night, his music helped her forget that too many things in reality don't make sense. And then, when she gets home, she'll give her old friend a call, see how things have been going.

When the piano is finally tuned she feels the way she always feels when she finishes tuning a piano: happy.

The Very Little Mouse

Tiny squeaks reach the ears of nine-year-old Leo. Out of curiosity—and vague concern—he picks up his pace. And then he sees, in the street, to his right, a very little mouse. Leo walks over to the mouse.

The mouse is trying to move, but struggling. The mouse takes two or three steps in one direction, then can't seem to go on. But then, after a few moments, he moves again, but this time in a different direction. For several painful minutes Leo watches the mouse, unpleasantly transfixed. Once in a while the mouse ends up on his back—with his soft belly exposed and paws waving around in the air—but manages to get himself turned the right way around. At this rate the mouse will be in the street all afternoon. These are the suburbs, and the street isn't busy, but eventually a car will probably run him over.

The mouse's squeaking is probably the worst part. It is fairly continuous.

The sun is big and bright. The pavement must be pretty hot today.

A car approaches. Leo makes sure to stand close to the mouse—putting a hand in the air—to ensure the mouse's safety. The car adjusts its course. If Leo hadn't been here, the car might have smooshed the mouse. The car disappears from view.

Leo checks his pockets. Empty. How can he get the mouse out of harm's way?

Leo tries to urge the mouse toward the sidewalk with a leaf, but it doesn't work.

Leo tries to pick up the mouse, but the mouse squirms around, terrified. Even though Leo can't see any teeth, he is afraid the mouse will bite him, so he abandons his attempt.

Home is not too far away, but it is far enough away to give a car more than enough time to cause irreparable damage.

Making sure no cars are coming, Leo makes his way over to the nearest house, glancing back every few steps to check on the traffic situation.

This is one of the more run-down houses in the neighborhood. An old woman lives here, he thinks, though he can't imagine what she looks like. With more than a little trepidation, he rings the doorbell.

"Excuse me," says Leo when the door is opened not by an old woman but by a middle-aged man wearing a cardigan. "Do you happen to have a couple of pieces of paper you could give me?"

"Sure." The man goes away and comes back, holding several sheets of paper.

Surprised the man hasn't asked any questions, Leo says, "There's a very little mouse I want to move out of the street. He's been squeaking. It's hard to watch… But he doesn't seem injured. I think he's just a baby and doesn't know what to do."

"I see. Well, good luck."

"Thanks."

Back in the street, Leo finds the mouse almost exactly where he left him. After a few moments he manages to get the mouse onto the paper, and carries him out of the street—making sure to hold the paper close to the ground, in case the mouse squirms off it.

Gently, Leo lowers the mouse onto some grass, in a shady spot. The mouse is still squeaking, but not as much. Hopefully he'll do better in the shade.

Leaving the mouse, Leo continues on his way to do what he'd been planning to do before hearing the tiny squeaks—which is to look at his friend's new bicycle. It turns out to be a very nice bicycle, and his friend lets him try it out, but the whole time Leo can't stop wondering about the mouse. Is he still squeaking? Will he be OK?

A couple of hours later, Leo is approaching the spot where he left the mouse. He so desperately hopes the mouse is OK that he almost doesn't want to investigate, since he is so scared about what he'll discover.

But he knows he must investigate.

And so, slowing his pace, he approaches the spot.

The very little mouse is still protected by the shade of the tree. The very little mouse's eyes are closed. The very little mouse is breathing gently.

Now Here

How did this life burst through this desolation? The silent monotony of sand—stretching out and farther out, seemingly ever farther out—has been punctured by a single joyous shriek of green. How?

In another time, in the same place, no sand is visible. Immense fronds, languorous, bob in the breeze. Fronds and fronds and fronds—some are brilliantly bright, emerald, and some are darker, deeper. In some small spaces, amid the green layers, fragments of water—a river? a lake?—transmit the light of the sun. And, almost close enough to touch, an ocelot leaps, moving from shadow to sun to shadow to sun to shadow in the space of a second. A gazillion tiny events allowed this motion to exist.

In another time, in the same place, bones and rings under earth under pavement under garbage are forgotten, while the Queen who ruled when these bones were surrounded by living flesh, when these rings transmitted the light of the sun, remains present in certain books and in the minds of the few who are interested in that particular obscure sliver of history. Having turned obscure, over centuries and centuries and centuries, because of its apparent absence of practical value.

In another time, in the same place, there is no place, and there is no time.

And now we are here. Knowing what now and here are—what *this* is—is not always a case of clarity. Fortunately we have been given, somehow, the opportunity to wonder.

Relief prevails.

Connecting Flights

The landing is not soft. That's OK. One can't—or shouldn't—expect every landing to be soft.

I unbuckle my seatbelt.

As the airplane moves along the tarmac I look out the oval window and pretend that everything out there is moving and that this airplane is motionless. Sometimes (often) it's fun to pretend.

Behind the airport the tops of tremendous white mountains have been consumed by clouds.

About fifteen minutes later my fellow passengers and I are walking down steps, onto the tarmac. It's very cold out—this is a winter day and we are at a high altitude—but it feels good to get fresh air after so much time in the airplane.

We are told to wait. A few buses should be here momentarily, we are told.

Some people are talking into their phones, and some people are looking at their phones, and some people are talking—in physical reality—to other people, and some of the people talking to other people in physical reality are simultaneously looking at their phones, and some people are doing—it seems—nothing. I am a member of the last group. (Although I *do* enjoy watching the figures my breathing makes in this very cold, high altitude winter air… So I guess one couldn't *actually* say I'm doing nothing.)

About five minutes later a few buses arrive. There's something strangely calming about trudging onto the bus: so often one has so many options to choose from that one experiences a frustrating indecisiveness—and sometimes, even, paralysis—but here, now, there is really only one reasonable option, which is to trudge onto this bus bound for Terminal B.

As I enter Terminal B I find myself automatically looking around for an informative blue screen. Before too long I find an informative blue screen, which informs me that my next flight is still on time. Which means I have one hour until boarding.

It isn't exactly easy to know what to do with this airport hour.

This is an odd in-between time.

I determine the direction of my gate, and walk in the opposite direction. I keep going until, eventually, my progress is blocked by a big wall of big windows. Through the windows I see, once again, those tremendous white mountains.

After looking at the mountains for a while I walk back the way I came.

At my gate I see that my flight is still on time.

Not nearly all of the seats in this area are occupied, but a woman in sweatpants is, nevertheless, sitting on the floor.

Instead of occupying one of the unoccupied seats, I continue walking until, eventually, I reach security.

There are so many people here, all around. Some people are going one way and some people are going another way and some people are going yet another way and some people aren't going anywhere at all.

There is a store not too far away—approximately forty feet—that sells popular books and magazines and souvenirs and food that supposedly isn't good for you. Inside the store I look at the covers of the magazines on display.

Back at my gate I see that my flight has been delayed.

This is extremely annoying.

I had no problem accepting the planned layover time, but I really hate it when things don't go according to plan. And I really don't want to spend more than an hour in this airport.

This is an odd in-between place.

My bag, which has been hanging on my right shoulder since I extracted it from the overhead bin, is starting to annoy me.

With a fresh cup of hot coffee in my left hand I walk back toward the windows that look out onto those tremendous white mountains. When I get to the windows I put my bag on the floor.

Standing there, occasionally taking a sip of coffee, I wish my flight weren't delayed, wish I could get where I'm going faster.

But at least this view isn't too bad.

Things could be worse.

Concealed Stars

The dog makes a sound.

Julia looks at the dog.

The dog makes a slightly different sound.

Julia detects a bit more humility in the second sound.

"OK," she says, and tosses her worn-down library book onto her worn-down coffee table. "Let's go."

Within seconds they're out the door. She doesn't bother to lock it; they'll surely be back within the hour, and this part of town has always seemed safe enough.

Expectantly, she turns her head to the sky to see the stars.

There are no stars.

It had been clear out when she returned home. But she can feel the wind now. Wind can change things pretty quickly.

At least it isn't too cold.

The dog begins to pee against a tree trunk. As a woman who values privacy, Julia turns away. When the dog is done, she'll review the site to confirm there isn't any fresh poop on the ground.

Julia and the dog continue their progress down the street. Nobody's around. Strange.

Crossing the intersection, they enter what Julia considers to be a different world.

Before crossing the intersection, the streetlights were modern; they emitted white, sterile light.

After crossing the intersection, the streetlights are old-timey, ornate; they gently, elegantly distribute rich golden tones.

One day, Julia tells herself, she'll move a few blocks and live among these lights of yesteryear. Live as a modern sculpture in a wing of antiquities.

It begins to rain. The dog hops a few times, thrilled. Julia isn't thrilled, but she certainly won't turn around yet. She had planned to go farther, so she will go farther. *And actually*, she thinks, *this rain is OK. And of course it wouldn't matter if I didn't think it was OK. It would still be raining.*

After another ten or so minutes of moving straight under light and steady rain, Julia and the dog turn right. They will loop back home.

The rain stops, unsurprisingly, right when they get back home.

Upon opening the door, Julia is surprised to see a woman in her apartment.

"The door wasn't locked," says the woman.

"I know."

"I got off early tonight."

"I can see."

"I thought I should make myself feel at home."

"Good," says Julia. "I'm glad you did."

Askin' Aspen

Aspen has worked at the radio station for three years—assisting show hosts with various aspects of their shows—and today it occurs to Mrs. Hammett that since Aspen has a nice voice and a nice personality, he himself could be a successful show host. She asks him if he's interested in the idea, and he nods. And then, for clarity, he says "Yes."

"What kind of show would you like to host?" says Mrs. Hammett.

Aspen thinks for a few moments. "I would like to host the kind of show where people with problems call in and ask for advice. I would like to give people good advice."

A few short weeks later, the show *Askin' Aspen* premieres. As Aspen starts to talk into the microphone—simultaneously entering countless cars and living rooms—he finds it very hard to believe that what is happening is actually happening. He has his own radio show! *Askin' Aspen*! Wow!

This new reality exceeds anything he had ever imagined for himself.

Everything seems wonderful—until the first caller starts talking.

"Thanks for taking my call," says the caller. "So my brother committed a terrible crime—I won't go into detail here—and I don't know what to tell my eight-year-old son. The thing is, my brother is a really terrific guy, and nobody ever expected him to do anything like this… But he did, there's a ton of evidence… But, so, my question: What should I tell my son?"

"What should you tell your son?" says Aspen.

"Yes, that's my question. He's used to seeing my brother fairly often, and he recently asked where my brother was… I didn't know what to say, so I changed the topic. But I need some kind of long-term plan here. Should I sit my son down and tell him the truth? Or should I wait for him to find out the truth on his own? Or should I invent a story that's more… palatable?"

"Well…" Aspen has no idea what to tell the caller. "Inventing a story would… Lying is generally bad… The truth is generally the best… But, then again, if this is a really terrible crime it could be very disturbing for your son… I guess that's obvious… Waiting for him to find out the truth on his own would definitely be the easiest solution… But maybe that wouldn't be the right solution?"

"I don't know. That's what I'm asking you."

"Well…"

Needless to say, Aspen fails to give the caller clear advice. When the call is over the caller still has no idea how to handle the situation.

Over the course of the rest of the show, Aspen takes many more calls. Aside from his answer to a question about carne asada tacos versus carnitas tacos, Aspen fails to give any caller any clear advice.

"I'm so sorry," he says to Mrs. Hammett after the show. "That was much harder than I'd expected."

"I thought you wanted to give people good advice," says Mrs. Hammett. "Why didn't you give people good advice?"

"Well… Whenever I had an idea about some advice to give, it seemed like there was other, contradictory advice that could possibly serve the caller better. It's hard to know what advice to give, and I suppose I would rather give no advice than the wrong advice."

Mrs. Hammett does not say anything, and looks displeased.

"Should we cancel the show? I would be happy to go back to my old job."

"I'll give you two weeks," says Mrs. Hammett. "Unless, that is, the show does not improve *at all* this week—in which case you'll only have one week."

The first person to call in to the following day's show is a high school senior who accidentally hit and killed the neighbor's dog with his car. As far as the caller knows, nobody saw it happen. And he hasn't told anyone about it until now.

He says he feels *extremely* guilty. He says he feels guilty even though he had been driving *extremely* carefully. He says he had been driving carefully when the dog unexpectedly—*extremely* unexpectedly—ran out into the street.

Here's where things get complicated. These particular neighbors have never gotten along with his parents, have disputed over trivial issues for years, and the caller is afraid that, if he tells the neighbors he killed their dog, relations will further deteriorate. Also, apparently, these particular neighbors are pretty loud and pretty intimidating: the caller is moderately worried about the emotional and physical consequences of a confession.

So what should he do? Confess and suffer the consequences? Or keep his mouth shut? He is asking Aspen.

"Well…" Aspen has no idea what to tell the caller. "It *seems* like the right thing to do is confess… They probably want to know what happened… They're probably very, very, *very* sad—that's how most people feel when their dog dies… But, then again, it seems like a confession could have pretty bad consequences not only for you, but also for your parents… And the dog is dead no matter what, a confession certainly won't change that, so maybe a confession is basically irrelevant? Probably it isn't irrelevant, actually… Not telling your neighbors what happened is essentially lying, and lying is generally bad… The truth is generally…"

Needless to say, Aspen fails to give the caller clear advice. When the call is over the caller still has no idea how to handle the situation.

Over the course of the rest of the show, Aspen takes many more calls. Aside from his answer to a question about the many benefits of good hydration, Aspen fails to give any caller any clear advice.

Over the course of the rest of the week, Aspen's advice-giving skills do not improve.

As he takes a seat across the desk from Mrs. Hammett, he fully expects to be told that *Askin' Aspen* will be canceled. Oh well. Things don't always work out.

"I have news for you," says Mrs. Hammett. "Your show gained listeners every day this week. We will not be canceling *Askin' Aspen*." She pauses. "Congratulations."

"But…" says Aspen. "Don't you think that, really, the show *should* be canceled? I mean, I almost never manage to give anyone good advice. The callers ask questions, and I don't have answers. I hate to say it, but it kind of seems like there's no good reason for me to be on the air."

"Where should I begin…? Alright. Considering your incompetence, your show's apparent success has puzzled me, so I've given the matter quite a bit of thought. My theory is that your inability to provide callers with clear advice does not actually annoy them; it actually *comforts* them. They call you because they don't know what to do about their problems, and the fact that you also don't know what should be done about their problems is possibly, for them, oddly comforting. You essentially confirm what most of them already knew, which is that their problems really *are* challenging and really *don't* have obvious answers. And so, when they are done talking with you, they understand that it's not unusual or pathetic to not quite know what to do. And so, they feel a little better—even if they still don't quite know what to do."

"Huh," says Aspen.

"And the *listeners* are entertained because it's always obvious that, yet again, you're not going to provide *any* clear advice. I think your incompetence amuses our listeners."

"Huh," says Aspen.

31

"So the show will go on," says Mrs. Hammett. "Alright. You can leave now."

New Views

Most of the ceiling is angled glass. Clean daylight establishes a pleasant simple mood and partly illuminates the thousands and thousands of objects in here. The other parts of an object can only be seen if the object is picked up and examined.

And that is exactly what the man does now. Turning the object around, it turns out that nothing about any of the exterior is in any way remarkable. Just another opaque thing, apparently. In a world replete with opacity. Unanswered questions.

But, when the man actually *opens* the object in his hands and focuses on what he sees within, something very strange happens: the room around him fades and the physical object itself fades and the examiner abruptly— and without even realizing it—loses all awareness of himself.

The examiner has entered a different world. His habitual mode of perception has been replaced with a new view. The shadows of clouds are lounging on soft green hills, and there's a woman who has finally decided to live with less restraint.

It isn't so easy to explain how these shadows and this woman arrived in this odd existence. The object in the examiner's hands is presenting symbols, which the examiner, strangely and essentially automatically, transfigures into a different world, with unique sounds and sights and emotions, with those shadows and that woman. And ideas also materialize—ideas and ideas and ideas. Some of the ideas are good. Some of the ideas are bad. Some of the ideas are unsettling in their ambiguity.

The examiner has lost all sense of time. Even though he is still standing and breathing under the glass ceiling, this object—and there are so, so, *so* many similar-looking objects all around, patiently waiting to share their own views—has transported him out of reality. But, whenever he finally does return to reality, it is quite possible that he will bring with him an interesting perspective that he found inside the object. Maybe he will even exit the object with some fresh empathy in his possession.

It is also quite possible that, while existing within the world of this object, he will become convinced that what has heretofore seemed important in life is, in fact, not. And that realization could be bad or good or good and bad. Almost certainly unsettling.

In any case, it is quite enjoyable right now, this transformance of symbols, this continuous creation of a world.

Eventually the examiner makes a decision: he goes over to the register to pay for the book.

A Very Good Plan

Kate will not let the rain win. When she makes a plan she plans to follow the plan. Of course she is willing to adapt to changes in circumstances and adjust a plan as necessary; and if circumstances change significantly enough to make an entire plan indisputably inadvisable, she will—albeit with great reluctance—discard the plan altogether.

Several days ago she and Marcus made a Saturday plan to go on a nice forty-seven-mile bike ride that will take them out of the city and along the coast. When they made the plan they agreed that it was a very good plan; but then the rain, which multiple meteorologists had said would start on Sunday, starts early Saturday, and though it can't be called a heavy rain it is certainly more than a light rain, and Marcus tells Kate he doesn't want to ride his bike in the rain—but maybe they can make a new plan for the day? Even though Kate no longer thinks the bike ride is a *very* good plan, she thinks it is still a good plan. Or, if not exactly a *good* plan, at least a *doable* plan. Which means that she wants to do it.

Kate will not let the rain win.

It's nine o'clock in the morning and the wet city streets, with their stretched reflections of car lights, are brighter than the sky. Kate, pedaling and drenched after only a few minutes, tells herself it's really great to be out here. Neither a computer screen nor a page is consuming her attention; walls and a roof are no longer protecting—*trapping!*—her body; instead she is free and in motion, out here, in the world. This is reality!

Kate is so glad she didn't let the rain win.

Coming to a stop at a red light, Kate places a foot on pavement. The rain, she notes, could now be called heavy. The top of her head feels odd because, while her helmet prevents rain from hitting *most* of the top of her head, there are a number of small openings in her helmet that allow rain to hit *some parts* of the top of her head; the lack of consistency is vaguely annoying. This odd annoyance hadn't bothered her while pedaling, though, and soon enough she will be out of the city and won't have any red lights to stop at for a long, long… long time. She's looking forward to that…

Pedaling again, glad to be back in motion—and another red light! The car next to Kate is playing her favorite Christmas song—but it's February. The man next to her, standing on the sidewalk under a big burgundy umbrella, is smoking a cigar. Heavy rain keeps falling. This is reality!

Less than fifteen minutes later Kate is back at home, having a hot shower.

The rain won. And Kate is glad, because now she is warm.

Hot Chocolate

Before too long a large green lake materializes, in the distance, on the other side of the window close to Daniel's eyes, and before too long this train is quite close to the large green lake, moving essentially parallel to the grass-covered shore, and before too long Daniel sees, in the distance, a long bridge going over the large green lake, and he wonders if there are railway tracks on the long bridge and, if so, if this train will, before too long, be rolling along those railway tracks, over that large green lake whose name, Daniel is embarrassed to admit to himself, he does not know. Though he knows where he came from and where he is going, he knows almost nothing about the waters and lands that lie between his point of departure and his destination.

Maybe this whole thing is, he considers, a mistake. Things had been going OK for him—certainly not *great*, but certainly OK—so why did he feel compelled to suddenly change everything about his life? Does he actually think he'll accomplish something worthwhile?

Well, he really doesn't know…

It is good for one to identify one's limitations and live within those limitations. The problem, Daniel supposes, is that it's hard to identify one's limitations from a safe distance: the identification of one's limitations must, inevitably, be accompanied by some kind of pain.

Daniel further supposes that he is, right now, in the early stages of crashing into the walls of his limitations. In the process of wrecking his life.

In an attempt to distract himself, he returns his attention to the things on the other side of the window—and he sees that he is still being moved alongside that large green lake, toward that long bridge. On the other side of the lake there is a big mountain with snow on the top third.

How high is the peak?

How deep is the lake?

Daniel looks at the woman sitting across from him. She has been there since he took his seat, but until now he hasn't paid her any attention. It appears as though she is in her early twenties—considerably younger than Daniel—and her dark, dark sunglasses totally conceal her eyes, and her hands are clasped together on her lap. Suddenly Daniel suspects that she has not moved her head—not even slightly—since he took his seat. She has not, he believes, looked at the view, has not looked at a book… Her face has, he believes, been directed at the empty seat next to him this whole time. Sure, she could be sleeping in an odd way… But he suspects that she is blind.

But then again, he certainly isn't certain.

Quite abruptly, he finds himself testing his theory: "It's"—he coughs to ensure attention—"This is a nice day, isn't it?"

"You're asking me?" says the woman with a crispness that makes it clear that she almost certainly had not been sleeping.

"Yes."

She swivels her head, and now her face is facing him. He really can't tell if she's blind or not. Her sunglasses really are impenetrable. "It is a nice day." She pauses. "But that isn't anything special: most days are nice." She pauses. "In one way or another."

"Ah."

Blind or not, this woman's attitude is clearly more appreciative than Daniel's. And if she *is*, in fact, blind… Well, if she is blind he should, he tells himself, feel ashamed of himself. Ashamed for not being sufficiently grateful for his own good optical luck.

In an attempt to distract himself, he returns his attention to the things on the other side of the window—and he sees that he is now being moved across the long bridge, over the large green lake. The bridge is quite low, which makes it easy for him to see the way the wind is moving the water.

"Excuse me," he says as he stands. He enters the aisle and moves to the next train car, and then to the next, and then to the next—at which point he is in the café car. He orders a hot chocolate at the counter and wonders how long it has been since he last drank a hot chocolate. It has definitely been quite a few years… And he has no idea why, just now, the overwhelming urge for hot chocolate arrived.

On his way back to his seat, with his hot chocolate in his left hand, he stops in the odd area between one train car and the next. Lifting the cup to his mouth, he takes a cautious sip.

This hot chocolate is very good.

He takes his second sip of hot chocolate.

Wonderful.

As a child he loved hot chocolate. Why, he wonders, did he stop drinking hot chocolate?

He makes a mental note to learn—or, he supposes, *re*learn—how to make a good hot chocolate. And maybe he will get into the habit of making a good hot chocolate every night before bed. That's the sort of habit, he considers, that has the potential to make day-to-day life a little bit better.

Looking out the little window of this odd in-between area, Daniel sees green water stretching out and, not too far out, a little island with some trees on it, and he remembers a wonderful photograph on the wall of the Indian restaurant they used to go to about once a month. The photograph showed a palace completely surrounded by water. A floating palace, essentially, elegant and at a dignified remove from the nearest prosaic land. Often, over the course of a meal at that Indian restaurant, Daniel would wonder about the history of that floating palace, wonder about how that floating palace was actually built, and he would plan to conduct some research about that floating palace. But he would always, upon leaving the Indian restaurant, forget all about the floating palace and his research plan; so he still hasn't gotten around to doing any floating palace research.

He now plans, yet again, to conduct floating palace research.

He takes his third sip of hot chocolate.

Wonderful.

How many miles until he reaches his destination?

How many miles has he already traveled?

He returns to his seat just as the possibly blind woman takes a big bite of apple. Listening to her chew, he doesn't think about anything in particular for the first time all day—and of course he doesn't realize that he isn't

43

thinking about anything in particular, and of course it is quite pleasant.

The woman lifts her right arm and begins to move her hand around on the window. The apple has been consumed to the core. Watching the uncertain movements of her hand, Daniel is now certain that she is blind. And she can't be more than twenty-five, which makes him feel sad. "Would you like me to open the window?"

"That would be helpful."

Reaching over, he lifts the latch and lowers the window about one foot, which is as far down as it will go.

She moves her right hand to where the fresh air is coming in and, with her left hand, throws the apple core out of the train. The core spins in the air, in the light of the sun—and then hits the water and goes under the surface.

"Thanks," says the woman. "You can close the window if you want. Or you can leave it open. Either way is fine with me."

Cross-Country Skiing

Somehow ten-year-old Leo got separated from the others.

The path he is skiing on is about to split into two paths. Since he does not know which way to go, he stops moving.

The others must not have realized that he fell behind. If they had, they surely would have waited here to make sure he goes the correct way.

In any case, he's here now, all alone, and he needs to make a decision.

Should he just wait here and hope that one of the others will come back here to show him the correct way?

Or should he guess which way is the correct way?

Or should he turn around and go back the way he came?

The problem with the last option is that they have been cross-country skiing for quite a while now, have covered a considerable distance, have made multiple turns… So Leo doesn't know if he would actually be able to find his way back.

The problem with the first option is that if he *does* wait here... Well, he has no idea how long it would take for one of the others to show up. Or, for that matter, if any of the others even *would* show up. Which is somewhat worrisome because we're on the verge of sunset.

Leo selects the middle option: he will guess which way is the correct way.

Supposedly he and the others were doing a big loop. Hopefully he is almost at the end of the big loop and will soon be back at the village.

But which way to go? Right or left?

Looking ahead, down both paths, it appears as though the forest is less dense around the path to the left. Maybe if Leo goes down that path the forest will soon end and he will soon be back at the village. Maybe the village is right around the corner.

Well, it turns out that the village is not right around the corner. But that's OK with Leo, because he enjoys moving his skis over the snow, and ever since the wind died down the air has felt pretty pleasant. And it's kind of exciting to be out here all on his own, with nobody to rely on other than himself.

But then he notices the sky. There really won't be too much light up there for too much longer...

Leo falls. He'd been skiing slightly downhill, picking up speed, and since he was so focused on the light in the sky he hadn't noticed an odd bump. And so, now, he is rolling off the path.

When he stops rolling he can immediately tell that he isn't hurt at all. Lying on the snow, he swivels his head and sees his skis lying on the snow several feet behind him, each at an odd angle. Sitting up, he crosses his legs and thinks. Should he keep going down that path or should he do something else?

He really doesn't know what to do.

He has always believed that he has pretty good instincts, but at the moment his instincts are telling him to do different things; they are not uniting to communicate a clear, single message.

Looking into the forest, Leo sees something different. Up until now pretty much everything has been trees and snow and sky and more trees. But this… This looks like some kind of rock formation.

Quickly on his feet, he begins to trudge through the snow, which is deeper and softer here than on the path. Within a minute he is standing at the entrance of a cave.

Leo hesitates—then enters the cave.

The sound of dripping reaches his ears, and he finds it simultaneously eerie and comforting.

And now rock, not snow, is underneath his feet.

Though he is moving forward slowly, the darkness is growing fast.

Approximately every seven or eight seconds he hears a very faint thud; it seems to be coming from deeper in the cave. He has no theories about the source of the very faint thud.

And now he can't see anything. It is simply too dark. He stops.

I'm going to take one more step, he thinks, *and then I'm going to turn around.*

He extends his foot—and hits something soft.

He returns his foot to its former position.

The very faint thud, he realizes, is coming from this soft thing.

Though his instincts are now united and telling him, clearly and in unison, to turn around and get out of this cave, his curiosity convinces him to ignore his instincts. He now has a theory, and he really wants to know if it's correct.

Taking off his right glove, he reaches down, reaches down… Fur!

Very soft fur.

This must be a hibernating bear, and the very faint thud must be the heartbeat.

Leo exits the cave.

And now, back on his skis, he decides to continue going in the same direction as before. After all, this direction has worked out pretty well so far. He touched a bear! That doesn't happen every day!

Cross-country skiing is, in Leo's opinion, significantly more satisfying than downhill skiing. When you're downhill skiing gravity is doing so much work for you, but when you're cross-country skiing so much depends on you yourself, on the effort that you as an individual are willing to exert. Cross-country skiing also feels kind of like a real journey. And it's nice to not have to wait around for the stupid gondola.

The sky is fairly orange now: night is right around the corner.

Leo sees, not too far away, a thin line of smoke going up into the orange sky: the village is close.

Unknowable Worlds

An unknowable world is perceived by the ant moving, all alone and at a fairly consistent pace, on the face of a monumental cliff, which is the leg of a chair. The house that houses the chair can't be discerned by the woman who is looking at the house, because she is looking at the house from a piece of metal thousands and thousands of feet away. The old man sitting on the front lawn of the house has lost almost all of his hearing and is unaware of the airplane above, and is also unaware, perhaps unsurprisingly, of the ant inside, moving on the chair leg that is a monumental cliff. A bird seizes the old man's attention by leaving its perch on the neighbor's tree. The old man watches the bird fly; and now the bird is a dot in the clear blue sky; and now the dot dissolves into the clear blue sky. Difference has been erased.

Now that the pleasant distraction that was the bird is gone, the old man resumes thinking about his granddaughter—and almost immediately interrupts himself. *Was that bird*, he wonders, *just a pleasant distraction? No, that isn't right at all. That bird was—is—as essential as anything else, and that which is essential can't be a distraction.*

Or... Or can it? He does not know, and resumes thinking about his granddaughter, who is moving far away to start a new life. He feels certain that she will come back to visit, and he feels certain that her visits will be rare and brief. Which is fine. She will build a life far away, and he will continue to do what he has been doing for years and years: start a new life right here, in the same exact place, every single day.

His granddaughter stops looking at the house she can't discern, turns from the small window to her work. So many things must be done. In order to meet her new employer's expectations. In order to prepare for all eventualities. In order to achieve sensational success. The people she has talked with so far seem nice enough— and that's nice. Is her wardrobe sufficient, or should it be expanded and enhanced? Looking out the small window again, at the infinitesimal indications of human life, at the less infinitesimal mountains over which this piece of metal will soon be flying, she thinks about how airplanes were used in the first world war barely one decade after an airplane's first successful flight. *What will your life*, she wonders, *be like in a decade? Wait—you're wondering about a decade from now? What will your life be like next week?* She does not know. Speculation is all that can really be done. Which is fine. Right now she is a breathing body among other breathing bodies—each of which creates its own

51

world—flying through the clear blue sky, thousands and thousands of feet above the earth, and it is all a bizarre miracle.

The solitary ant is no longer on the leg of the chair, but on a vast plain. No other life can be seen. He keeps moving. Though the world this ant perceives is unknowable, it does not seem too unreasonable to suspect that he is trying to figure something out. But who knows? What is known is that this ant keeps moving across the living room carpet, this vast plain, at a fairly consistent pace, and all alone—until, at long last, he finds another ant.

Orange Soda

The homeless man's face is so dirty that it's hard to tell, but he seems to be about my age. As I get closer he stands up and holds out a styrofoam cup. Nobody else is around.

With a slightly tilted head he says, not in an asking-for-money tone but in a posing-a-profound-philosophical-question tone, "What is do that?"

Though the question does not make sense, I think I understand what he's saying. *How did this—me living on the street like this—happen? And how can fate be flipped? There are certain things one wants to do—but what are the limits of control?*

That's what I imagine, anyhow. I have no idea how far from reality I am.

Standing here opposite him, I have no idea why I'm standing here opposite him, since I can't help him. Well, I could give him some change, or even a few dollars—but I know I'm not going to give him any money, because I know how easy it will be to not give him any money and not feel any worse about myself. What makes it easy is the not unlikely possibility that he would use the money on drugs.

But even if I had some guarantee that he wouldn't use the money on drugs, it still wouldn't be fair to give him any money: there are many, many homeless people asking for money in this city, and it doesn't seem fair to give money to one and none of the others—and if I start giving money to every homeless person I come across, I'll run out of money for myself.

I give him an apathetic "Sorry" and continue on my way.

Many hours later, after leaving work, the summer sun hits me a certain way and I want water. Conveniently there is a convenience store right here. While opening a refrigerator door and reaching for a bottle of water, I notice orange soda behind the neighboring refrigerator door—and without any thought I open the neighboring refrigerator door and grab a cold can of orange soda while the first refrigerator door swings—very, very slowly—shut.

Desperate for water and then desperate for orange soda. It's pretty strange, when you think about it, how one minute you can really want one thing and the next minute—next second, really—you really want a very different thing. Your whole world changes in the space of a second.

What's also strange about this recent development is the fact that I don't even drink orange soda. Or haven't in years, anyhow. I used to drink a lot of orange soda, but shortly after college I quit all sodas. Until now, apparently.

Walking along the sidewalk, sipping a wonderful orange soda, clear images of Europe arrive, memories of summer holidays when we would see justifiably famous works of art, when we would climb to the tops of grand old churches, when we would swim in the Mediterranean, when we would walk along linden-dotted sidewalks, when I would often be holding an orange soda with the same hand with which I'm holding an orange soda now—though I once heard that almost no cells in the human body last longer than seven years before being replaced, and those fortunate childhood summers happened longer ago than that, so maybe the hand I have now isn't actually the same hand—and there he is again, just ahead, and I kind of wish I were walking on the other side of the street, or had taken a different route altogether.

This time the homeless man doesn't stand up, but remains cross-legged on the concrete with his back against a building. The styrofoam cup is no longer in his hand, but on the concrete, and I see written on it, in big black letters, "HELP." His hand must have been covering that word earlier—and now his hand is holding something else: a can of orange soda.

His can of orange soda is identical to my can of orange soda, and I wonder if his parents used to take him to Europe for summer vacation.

That sudden unexpected overwhelming desire, back in that convenience store, for orange soda was…

Standing here opposite him, I have no idea why I'm standing here opposite him, since I can't help him. Or… can I help him? Is there a way for me, as an individual, to actually make a positive difference in the trajectory of this man's life? He likes orange soda and I like orange soda. How easily could I be in his position?

My awareness of our shared affinity for orange soda moves me to not move from this spot until I figure out some way to help him. While thinking hard and trying to be logical, I realize the homeless man is saying something—as soon as I transfer my attention from thoughts to him, he stops talking. Though I'm guessing he was just talking gibberish again, I say, just in case, "Sorry—I missed that. What?"

He lifts his can of orange soda a few inches and says, with his surprisingly clear eyes connecting with my eyes, "They put way too much sugar in this stuff."

Evening Exploration

The little dog is ambling along a suburban street. He does not know where he came from, does not know where he is going, does not know why he is here, right now, ambling along this suburban street. His current suburban-street existence is enfolded in mysteries he would never think about thinking about.

There is no longer much light in the sky. But below the sky, every now and then, to the little dog's left and right, bright lights materialize.

Options are not really an option for this little dog: in every moment there is something he senses he should do, and he always instantly proceeds to do whatever that something happens to be. And so, right now, he trots off the street and into a yard in which a light is illuminating a cactus.

The little dog examines the cactus. Moving his nose perilously close to the cactus's needles, he sniffs.

Hmm…

He sniffs again.

Interesting.

Trotting back into the street, the little dog continues his journey in the same general direction as before, toward a future whose contents he would never think about thinking about.

And now yet another light materializes. But, unlike the other lights, this new light is moving. Instinctively, the little dog starts sprinting toward this new light. What could it be?

Just when the little dog is getting really close to the new light, a monumental screech fills his ears. Instinctively, the little dog stops moving. The light has stopped moving. The little dog barks at the light. Then, with some caution, the little dog approaches the light.

The little dog examines the light. Moving his nose close to the light, he sniffs.

Hmm...

He sniffs again.

Interesting.

Turning to continue his journey, the little dog is suddenly facing a woman who is partly illuminated by the light.

And now the little dog notices a scent that is very, *very* familiar. It's... Yes! The little dog recognizes this woman! The little dog *knows* this woman!

The woman picks up the little dog, brings him close to her face, and says some words. The little dog does not understand what the woman is saying, but he is happy to be here, so high in the air. It's fun.

Instinctively, the little dog licks the woman's nose.

The Mystery Philosophy Of The Octopus

When the lab is dark and all of the humans are gone, the octopus uses several of his arms to push open the lid of his tank. After lifting himself up to the rim— where he positions himself firmly, so he won't fall onto the floor—he uses several of his arms to open the lid of the neighboring tank. Immersing himself in the new environment, his eight arms spread out like a flower suddenly blooming—then snap together around a fish. When he finishes his dinner he returns to his own tank— and makes sure to close the lids of both tanks, so that no humans will know about his nocturnal activities, which are really none of their business.

Across the planet, in another lab, an octopus hates one of the lab workers. All of the other workers are fine, but this guy… There's just something about him that she can't stand. Even though all of the workers wear identical uniforms, she always knows when the one she hates is approaching—and, when he is close enough, she fires a jet of water at his head. That worker now avoids her as much as he can, but sometimes his responsibilities give him no choice but to get close to her tank. He has grown to hate her because, as far as he can tell, her hatred of him is not in any way justified. So this is yet another example of something that, sadly, shows no sign of ever stopping: hate inspiring hate.

But octopuses can also be affable; some are even renowned for their wonderful ocean hospitality. About a year ago I was dining with an old friend, who told me she had encountered an octopus while scuba diving off the coast of Australia. Before this conversation I had never given octopuses much thought, and when Laura began her story I was not instantly interested in what she was saying, and was partly thinking about something else— but then the octopus grabbed her hand, and with it my full attention. After some gentle urging Laura agreed to go along with the octopus, though she had no idea where they were going or why.

Laura was maintaining awareness of her oxygen level and of time—but it seemed like her watch was lying to her. Seconds were expanding far beyond their standard definition. Each second refused to end until it was ready to end. Maybe this should not be too surprising, as she was fairly far from the surface and swimming, arm in arm, with an octopus. An octopus whose intentions were unknown! And so several days passed in eleven minutes—at which point Laura and the octopus arrived at a small outcrop, next to which were some piles of stones and shells and pieces of glass. The octopus gestured to one particular area, where there was a collection of shiny objects: emeralds and silver spoons and an enormous sapphire and quite a few doubloons. "It was a very nice little hideaway," said Laura. "I felt happy and safe there. He was a delightful host."

Across the planet, in another ocean, an octopus comes across a half-buried half of a coconut shell. He fires jets of water around the edges of the shell, to loosen the shell from the mud, then pulls the shell out of the mud. Then he fires more jets of water at the shell, to thoroughly clean the shell. Then he positions the shell just under the center of his body, with the concave side facing up, so that the shell almost fits with his body and won't cause too much additional water resistance. Then he starts to walk, a bit awkwardly, along the seabed.

Over the next hour and a half the octopus comes across more halves of coconut shells, and with each shell repeats the process described above. Eventually, when he has a respectable stack of seven shells, he stops at a nice little cave and begins to place the shells around the entrance. Earlier today this octopus must have finally decided it was time for him to have his own little home—and then he formulated a plan, and then he started to execute the plan.

Another octopus swimming about, in a far-flung green-blue fraction of the planet, has numerous predators—including those barbaric blue sharks—and keeps her eyes open for fragments of venomous tentacles that were once attached to a Portuguese man o' war; because this octopus is immune, and those barbaric blue sharks are not. Whenever possible, this octopus carries around these venomous tentacle fragments—even though it really is a hassle. The fact that self-preservation is not at all easy, and requires so much daily effort, can be really frustrating.

According to certain scientists, the most recent ancestor we shared with octopuses existed about six hundred million years ago: octopuses' intelligence is tremendously different from our intelligence. And since octopuses have been around for much longer than humans—supposedly more than one thousand times longer—one wonders if they possess some deep knowledge, some kind of comprehension of the world, that we lack. Have they developed a philosophy that we would find—if they could just clearly communicate it to us—profound and enlightening? Surely it's at least *possible* that they have been pondering something supreme down there, beneath the waves, while we have been focusing on money and technology and art and war. What secrets are hidden in their mystery philosophy?

Sadly, we may never be able to answer that question.

While everything I've written about octopuses up to this point has been based on things I've heard and read, I actually have had several of my own meaningful encounters with octopuses. And I can honestly report that I have found them to be very tender creatures. When cooked properly, there is really nothing like them. And the octopus they serve here, in this little restaurant in this calm city on the edge of Europe, on this calm summer day, could not be better.

A Vacation

They put a tent and a couple of sleeping bags into the trunk and drive off—with no destination in mind.

They don't even look at a map. They head, generally, west, but when they see a sign for a place with an intriguing-sounding name, they sometimes follow the sign, even if it means going north or south for a while.

Many small towns are seen. A few cities are seen. A lot of countryside is seen.

When stopping in certain places they learn things they had never expected to learn—and which, in all likelihood, they will one day forget.

Occasionally they think about taking photographs. To ensure the preservation of memories.

But they never take any photographs. For some reason they sense they would never actually look at the photographs... So why bother taking the photographs in the first place?

In future years, having not taken any photographs may be a regret.

In future years, having not taken any photographs may not be a regret.

Who knows how decisions made today will look from future years?

They always find a reasonable place to install their tent by mid-afternoon. Then they go for a long walk around wherever they happen to be. Which sometimes isn't quite known.

When it's getting dark they make a fire and use its light to read and play backgammon and see the food they eat.

And a lot of the time they just watch the fire burn and talk about this or that or nothing.

This journey won't last too long. They have obligations to which they must, before too long, return. But those obligations, whenever they think about them as the days pass, feel increasingly foreign. Certainly not *bad*... simply foreign.

For the most part, though, they feel like they are truly living in the present. When they're driving along and see an intriguing-looking lake or river, they sometimes stop the car and go for a swim in the intriguing-looking lake or river. Which is very nice.

And tonight they are camping right next to a lake. The stars are very bright and there is no wind, so they can easily see the reflection of the stars on the surface of the water. They probably spend more time looking at the reflection of the stars than at the stars themselves.

The next morning they find themselves in a tiny town with one diner. They park the car and go into the diner. A friendly waitress comes over to their table and asks them what they would like. A coffee and a waffle for one and an orange juice and scrambled eggs for the other.

It turns out to be a very good breakfast.

As they eat, they realize it's time to start driving back home.

They're looking forward to the journey back.

They're also looking forward to when the journey back is over.

It will be very nice to sleep inside again.

Honey Laughs A Lot

When Honey wakes up in the morning it often takes him a few moments to remember where he is and what his life is like—and as soon as he remembers, he can't help but chuckle. Because he has his wife next to him. Because the day he's about to enter doesn't seem too bad at all.

When Honey puts on his uniform and looks at himself in the mirror, he can't help but chuckle. This is how he has turned out! Since he really can't imagine a better alternative, he chuckles again.

And when Honey steers that big city bus out of the depot and onto the street, he absolutely loves his height and vantage point, and chuckles again.

He loves listening to his passengers. They say so many funny things! Generally, he realized a few years back, people take their lives very, very seriously. But that doesn't mean Honey has to!

Since he starts driving quite early in the morning, he gets off at 3. Usually, after getting back to his neighborhood, he goes to the diner and eats a slice of pecan pie.

He leisurely enjoys his pie, and sometimes follows it with a leisurely stroll around the neighborhood, but always makes sure to be back at his apartment by 5—at which point he places himself in the comfortable chair by the window and looks out at the street.

Because, at almost exactly 5:04 every day, an oldish man on a bicycle rides by. The cyclist always wears the same outfit: white shoes, short white shorts, a white sweater, and a big white football helmet that looks like it's from 1970. The combination of the outfit and the determined, uncompromising expression on the cyclist's face makes Honey laugh.

And by 5:20 another treat arrives. A youngish, shirtless, shoeless man wearing black pants walks down the street, very slowly, while making a four-foot-long stick do the most remarkable things. He spins the stick all around. He throws the stick in the air. He occasionally hits himself with the stick. Like the cyclist, the stick guy always looks serious. The stick guy is clearly totally devoted to his craft. The fact that it is such an odd craft makes Honey laugh.

One day while Honey's driving the bus he hears two passengers meet unexpectedly. It's quickly apparent to Honey that these people have not met for many, many years. Since college, it seems. The man asks questions. Though the woman is clearly reluctant to answer his questions, she does—but as concisely as possible. Well, she was married, but her husband died. Well, she had the comfort of two children, but both were killed—one by a war and one by a drunk driver. Though she had had a decent career, she eventually reached a certain point... and just couldn't maintain focus.

As the woman speaks, tears emerge from Honey's eyes. This isn't funny at all. And the fact that the woman doesn't tell her story with self-pity, but rather matter-of-factness, makes Honey even sadder.

For the rest of his shift he doesn't laugh at all. He drives with a stony face.

Considering his mood, it probably isn't too surprising that he skips his customary afternoon slice of pecan pie.

Back in his apartment he sits on the floor. Maybe, he thinks, he hasn't been taking things seriously enough.

After sitting there for quite some time, he notices the clock on the wall. 5:03. He gets to his feet and goes over to the window. And out there, just coming into view, is the cyclist with the big white football helmet—and he's as determined as ever.

Honey smiles.

And then, a few minutes later, the stick guy arrives—and he's moving the stick around with all of his usual energy and flair.

Honey smiles again.

Tomorrow, Honey decides, he'll stop the cyclist and tell him that he appreciates his work. And then he'll stop the stick guy and tell him that he appreciates *his* work.

But the next day, while he's driving the bus, he cancels his plan. His concern is that if he says those things to the cyclist and the stick guy, they may think he's making fun of them.

But that isn't what he would have been doing at all: he genuinely appreciates their work and would like to thank them.

Because they had helped him smile again.

When The Moon Bounces

The night is not inviting.

Alice opens the front door. Cold air blows against her. She closes the front door. She hadn't intended to go out anyway. She had simply been curious.

Less than two minutes later she's moving down the sidewalk. After all, she figures, she is only a visitor here. So, since she will only be here for a short while, oughtn't she make the most of here while she can?

Though she had hoped Brian would join her on her walk, she wasn't at all surprised when he said he would prefer to stay inside the cottage. Where it is warm.

Well, that's fine with her. She doesn't mind walking alone.

But it is certainly cold. That is undeniable.

And it is certainly windy. That is also undeniable.

But it is good, as usual, to be in motion.

And those sounds are quite nice—those sounds, to her left, of waves crashing, again and again and again, into rocks. Imagine those waves slowly, so slowly, wearing down those rocks, forcing them, over millennia, into new shapes. One's context, thinks Alice, determines so much.

She decides to think about something else—and does start thinking about something else. For a long time it was very difficult for her to decide to think about something else and actually succeed in thinking about something else, but over time she has honed that ability.

Light is emerging from the window of a house just ahead, to her right. Making sure that her steps aren't making any noise, she goes over to the edge of the window and looks in.

An upright piano. An old green lamp—which is what allows her to see things. Books on shelves—but they're too far away to read the titles. Nobody is in the room.

Alice wonders if the piano is in or out of tune.

A deer clatters down the street, seizing Alice's attention.

Ahead there's a little turn, and the rocky coast is replaced by a beach with fine sand. Steps lead Alice down to the sand. As her shoes touch sand, she sees a suspended tennis ball.

No: it's the moon. Yellow and almost full. The light it's throwing down reveals how rough the water is tonight.

Very rough.

She'd always believed she would have a successful tennis career. She'd been pretty close, for a while. But her body proved itself to be insufficiently durable.

Life had not aligned itself with her plans. Oh well.

Eyes on the moon, she watches it fall, approach the horizon, hit the horizon, and bounce back up to its former position. She sits on the sand, puts her arms around her knees, and watches the moon bounce—again and again and again.

It is time, she decides, to figure out her future.

She decides that whenever she stands up she'll go straight back to the cottage and have a nice hot shower. And then she'll make some tea. And then maybe she and Brian will talk about something. Or maybe she'll continue reading her book. Or maybe she'll play her guitar.

Though she isn't exactly sure what she'll do, she's glad she has options.

The Admiral

They had moved. Again.

It wasn't easy to get a sense of things. Suddenly everyone was different, and Leo felt like he didn't have enough time to figure out who these people were. He felt adrift.

"Don't talk to The Admiral." That's one of the first things his father told him after they moved into the apartment complex.

Nobody really knew what was going on with The Admiral. Nobody even knew if he had ever actually *been* an admiral. Yes, he wore the kind of uniform one would expect an admiral to wear (deep blue, always crisp, with the buttons always polished, shining), but whenever he spoke—which, admittedly, was seldom, possibly because everyone tried to keep their distance from him—he spoke coarsely. Like a pirate.

It was confusing.

In the center of the apartment complex was an oval pool. The Admiral was by far the biggest user of the pool.

But he never got wet.

The Admiral had a plastic raft. From his apartment on the second floor he would carry the raft down the stairs, walk over to the edge of the pool, and drop the raft onto the water. Then he would get onto the raft—while still wearing that crisp, deep blue uniform with polished, shining buttons.

And he would stay there, on that raft, for hours. And just float around the pool. Sometimes he read a newspaper. Sometimes he kept his eyes on the sky. And sometimes he simply slept.

Though nobody *actually* knew, pretty much everyone in the apartment complex assumed The Admiral was a drunk. How else could you explain why a distinguished-looking, elderly man was spending so much time lying, fully dressed, on a plastic raft in a pool?

At this point in the story, with the descriptions I've provided, you probably think The Admiral had a big belly.

Well, he didn't. He was, in fact, astonishingly compact.

Leo was intrigued the moment he first saw The Admiral. He had never seen that kind of uniform before. And, while many people could say many things about The Admiral, nobody could say he didn't take terrific care of his uniform. It always looked so perfectly crisp. The buttons always looked so perfectly polished; they always shined. And that deep blue was so… dignified.

The contradictions of The Admiral, Leo sensed within his first few weeks at the apartment complex, were many.

Unlike many kids his age, Leo's father let him walk home from school on his own. When he arrived at the apartment complex in the afternoon, he would always go slightly out of his way to get back to their apartment: he would walk by the pool to see if The Admiral was there. On his raft. Wearing his shiny crispy blue uniform.

Right when Leo saw The Admiral, on this particular day, a big gust of wind blew the newspaper off his chest.

The newspaper flew high into the air, then swirled down onto concrete, quite a ways away. The pages were fluttering wildly, threatening to disperse.

Some pages dispersed.

A desperate howl burst out of The Admiral.

As if ordered into battle, Leo ran and proceeded to collect the pages. Before walking over to the edge of the pool to hand them to The Admiral, he made sure they were in the proper order.

"Thank ye, lad," said The Admiral in his coarse pirate growl.

"You're welcome," said Leo.

The Admiral opened the newspaper and looked at it. Leo couldn't tell if he was actually reading it.

Knowing his father would want him to walk away, Leo said, "How long have you been doing this?"

"Aargh," said The Admiral, without looking up from the newspaper. "Judging by the light, I'd wager it's going on three hours now. Aargh."

"I meant… How long have you been using your raft thing in this pool?"

The Admiral turned from the newspaper to Leo. "Well, I suppose I would have to say that it has probably been *too* long." Leo noticed that The Admiral wasn't talking like a pirate anymore. "It has not been easy to figure out what to do after leaving the sea."

"You don't sound like a pirate anymore."

The Admiral didn't say anything for a few moments. It looked like he was about to cry. Then he smiled. "Thank you."

"For what?"

"Noticing."

Get Back

The sun shines on gravestones. Bells in the bell tower clang. Wind moves new leaves, not one of which releases its grip.

School is out. Some boys and girls are hanging around, some standing on overgrown grass and some sitting on the low stone wall that separates this little church graveyard from the street below. Laughter and stories and smoke are in the air. Each kid tries to impress the others, but it all seems natural and not inauthentic. They are entertaining each other. They are filling space that could otherwise feel empty.

This is happening in the present, but this is also happening—albeit in distorted fashion—in the mind of the old man sitting on the same low stone wall, alone in a grey mist, decades and decades after what was just described as the present, very far away from those fresh young faces in motion. Strange: between then and now no time has passed and eternity has passed. At least that's how it feels.

Back then the future was frequently a vague and significant concern. What to do with it? With all that time and all those unknown spaces ahead, countless mysteries... Too often the future manages to feel almost unbearably important—until a moment arrives in which someone, in this case one of the kids sitting on the low stone wall, says something unexpectedly comforting. The future still hasn't arrived, and who knows if it ever will arrive, so what's the point of worrying about it now? Maybe the future will get lost somewhere and won't be able to find us.

But there is one future that looks good to the boys in the little church graveyard: music. But will music allow them to live well? Are they even wondering about that right now? Or are they just trying to enjoy what can be enjoyed, just trying to make the most of the present, just trying to have fun playing music when they can? Or is there a fanatical drive within those boys—to get themselves out of this town, to create wonderful songs, to earn fortunes, to be known by all?

Though he tries, the old man in the grey mist is unable to remember exactly what they were thinking.

And *why* did what happened happen the way it happened?

The most appealing explanation is difficult to prove.

But at least the old man does clearly remember— or at least *thinks* he clearly remembers, which is probably good enough—that one particular adolescent spring afternoon in the graveyard, those clanging bells, his now-long-dead friend telling about how he recently fell out of his favorite tree, the sunlight on the gravestones, the laughter and the smoke, himself telling about how he was locked out of his house and had to climb in through the bathroom window because he missed dinner again, the bright green leaves, the way she looked and the way she was looking at him, the breeze.

Here's what those boys did after they left that little church graveyard: Across The Universe All I've Got To Do All My Loving All Together Now All You Need Is Love And I Love Her And Your Bird Can Sing Another Girl Any Time At All Ask Me Why Baby, You're A Rich Man Baby's In Black Back In The U.S.S.R The Ballad Of John And Yoko Because Being For The Benefit Of Mr. Kite! Birthday Blackbird Blue Jay Way Can't Buy Me Love Carry That Weight Come Together The Continuing Story Of Bungalow Bill Cry Baby Cry A Day In The Life Day Tripper Dear Prudence Dig A Pony Dig It Do You Want To Know A Secret? Doctor Robert Don't Bother Me Don't Let Me Down Don't Pass Me By Drive My Car Eight Days A Week Eleanor Rigby The End Every Little Thing Everybody's Got Something To Hide Except Me And My Monkey Fixing A Hole Flying The Fool On The Hill For No One For You Blue From

Me To You Get Back Getting Better Girl Glass Onion Golden Slumbers Good Day Sunshine Good Morning Good Morning Good Night Got To Get You Into My Life Happiness Is A Warm Gun A Hard Day's Night Hello, Goodbye Help! Helter Skelter Her Majesty Here Comes The Sun Here, There, And Everywhere Hey Bulldog Hey Jude Hold Me Tight Honey Pie I Am The Walrus I Call Your Name I Don't Want To Spoil The Party I Feel Fine I Me Mine I Need You I Saw Her Standing There I Should Have Known Better I Wanna Be Your Man I Want To Hold Your Hand I Want To Tell You I Want You (She's So Heavy) I Will If I Fell If I Needed Someone I'll Be Back I'll Cry Instead I'll Follow The Sun I'll Get You I'm A Loser I'm Down I'm Happy Just To Dance With You I'm Looking Through You I'm Only Sleeping I'm So Tired I've Got A Feeling I've Just Seen A Face In My Life The Inner Light It Won't Be Long It's All Too Much It's Only Love Julia Lady Madonna Let It Be Little Child The Long And Winding Road Long, Long, Long Love Me Do Love You To Lovely Rita Lucy In The Sky With Diamonds Magical Mystery Tour Martha My Dear Maxwell's Silver Hammer Mean Mr. Mustard Michelle Misery Mother Nature's Son The Night Before No Reply Norwegian Wood (This Bird Has Flown) Not A Second Time Nowhere Man Ob-La-Di, Ob-La-Da Octopus's Garden

Oh! Darling Old Brown Shoe One After 909 Only A
Northern Song Paperback Writer Penny Lane Piggies
Please Please Me Polythene Pam P.S. I Love You Rain
Revolution 1 Revolution 9 Rocky Raccoon Run For
Your Life Savoy Truffle Sexy Sadie Sgt. Pepper's Lonely
Hearts Club Band She Came In Through The Bathroom
Window She Loves You She Said She Said She's A
Woman She's Leaving Home Something Strawberry
Fields Forever Sun King Taxman Tell Me What You See
Tell Me Why Thank You Girl There's A Place Things
We Said Today Think For Yourself This Boy Ticket To
Ride Tomorrow Never Knows Two Of Us Wait We Can
Work It Out What Goes On What You're Doing When I
Get Home When I'm Sixty-Four While My Guitar
Gently Weeps Why Don't We Do It In The Road? Wild
Honey Pie With A Little Help From My Friends Within
You Without You The Word Yellow Submarine Yer
Blues Yes It Is Yesterday You Can't Do That You Know
My Name (Look Up The Number) You Like Me Too
Much You Never Give Me Your Money You Won't See
Me Your Mother Should Know You're Going To Lose
That Girl You've Got To Hide Your Love Away.

Bells in the bell tower are clanging in the past and
in the present. The old man stands and notices that the
sun is trying to come out, trying to break through the grey
mist. It has been a long cold lonely winter. He is still

hearing his friend's voice, from all those years ago but as clear as anything in this current cold reality, talking about falling out of that tree. Since then the old man has lived many afternoons that were as enjoyable as that adolescent spring afternoon, but he doesn't think he ever lived an afternoon that was better.

Special

Driving through yet another run-down town, Alice is beginning to wish she had flown. She had thought it would be fun to see a part of the country she had never seen before, but it has mostly been depressing. There have simply been too many run-down towns on her route. And how, she wonders, did people actually end up out here?

Alice supposes that each person who decided to move out here was motivated by some form of optimism. Which is a shame. For Alice has learned, through her own experiences, that optimism can be quite dangerous.

Alice has been quite hungry for almost an hour now, and no reasonable food option has presented itself. The last two restaurants she saw were boarded up, clearly abandoned.

Why didn't she bring along some apples or something? Why did she bring nothing? Yes, tonight's rehearsal dinner will almost certainly be substantial… But she'll definitely need to eat at least *something* before then!

Alice is so busy berating herself for not bringing along a single snack that she almost doesn't notice Alice's Café. *Alice's* Café? What are the chances?

Though Alice's Café looks almost as run-down as the rest of the town, its windows are not boarded up and a sign on the door says "OPEN."

Alice is relieved to have finally found food.

Pulling off the road, she plans to get back on the road as quickly as possible.

And now her eyes are slowly adjusting from the cloudless day to the dim interior. Eight tables of worn-down wood are scattered around; two are occupied. A wide opening in the wall opposite the entrance allows Alice to see the top halves of an old man and a young woman moving around in the kitchen. Noticing Alice standing in the entrance, the old man smiles and says "Sit anywhere. I'll be with you in a minute."

Alice sits at a table in a corner, in a chair that gives her a good view of the whole interior. The other patrons are, at one table, two men who appear to work in construction and, at another table, a heavily tattooed woman and a little boy.

The old man places a menu and a glass of water in front of Alice. "Anything to drink?"

"Black coffee, please."

Reviewing the menu, Alice is surprised—and, frankly, a bit overwhelmed—by the number of options. She can't quite figure out what she's in the mood for. She closes the menu.

She opens the menu when the old man comes over with the coffee. "Do you think this is a good sandwich?" she says, placing her right index finger next to an item on the menu.

"I would advise against it. I recommend the house special," he says, placing his right index finger next to a different item on the menu.

Rereading the description of the house special, it again looks like something she probably wouldn't enjoy. But she appreciates the old man's candor, and decides to follow his advice.

There's no music playing and Alice can easily hear the conversations of the other patrons—but she doesn't listen to them. Instead she listens to the cooking sounds coming from the kitchen.

Remembering her coffee, she looks at it. Steam is rising and twirling in the air.

Alice lifts the mug and takes a sip.

The coffee tastes extremely good.

"The house special," says the old man, placing a plate in front of Alice. And he adds, before walking away, "I hope you like it."

Alice gets some food onto the fork and takes a bite.

The house special tastes extremely good.

For several bites she focuses exclusively on the bites, on the excellence of this food.

And then she begins to think about the future. When she leaves this place she will drive another hundred or so miles. Then she'll check into the hotel, get settled, and eventually go to the rehearsal. And then, tomorrow, the wedding will happen. Though she wishes she weren't attending alone, she's pretty sure she'll find a way to have a good time.

"What do you think?" says the old man, whose approach Alice had not noticed.

"It's wonderful," says Alice.

"Good," says the old man. He pours more coffee into her mug. "Do you want anything else?" She shakes her head. "Well here's the bill. But please don't rush. Stay as long as you like."

The old man walks away.

Stay as long as you like. What a nice thing to say.

This really isn't a bad place.

This really is a very good place.

As Alice swallows the final remnant of the house special, she notices an upright piano on the other side of the room. She wonders if it has not been played in years and is wildly out of tune, or if it is played frequently and tuned on a regular basis.

Stay as long as you like.

Alice leans back in her chair, takes a sip of coffee, looks down at the worn-down wood of the table, and smiles.

Golden Old Rusty Dumpster

On the surfaces of the lands are larches and ladybugs and limousines and lovers and libraries and impending liftoffs.

Some of the liftoffs are destined to land in places you have known or will someday know.

Some of the liftoffs are destined to land in places you have never known and will never know.

The old rusty dumpster is illuminated by sunlight. The child is old enough to understand this. But something about the quality of the light on the dumpster makes the light appear as though it is somehow embedded in the dumpster. Or as though the dumpster is somehow generating the light itself.

This is oddly beautiful.

Under the surfaces of the waters are porpoises and plastics and piranhas and propellers and plateaus.

Most of the underwater plateaus have never been seen by human eyes.

The child moves his attention away from the golden old rusty dumpster. Several barges are in the canal. What would it be like, he wonders, to live on a barge?

When it comes to ways to live, there are so many possibilities.

Though, maybe, the child sadly considers, not every possibility is actually a possibility for every person.

Above the surfaces of the lands and waters are helicopters and high jumpers and hawks and honeybees and hot air balloons.

Some of the journeys above the surfaces will be long.

Some of the journeys above the surfaces will be short.

As the child, back on his bicycle, moves through time and space, everything seems simple.

A nice breeze.

A nice memory of a golden old rusty dumpster.

Ragtime Afternoon

Music is drifting into the inside from the outside, mostly through the open second-floor window. It could easily be a window that slides open, but let's make it a window that opens outward, toward the rest of the world. Our protagonist, sitting at his desk, is listening to the music, which is Bach played on a guitar. The player's technique is remarkable, but the guitar is wildly out of tune. The sun shines through the solar system, shines through our planet's atmosphere, shines through the gap between the wall and the window, shines into the eyes of our protagonist. The sun is also making two shapes on the desk. One of the shapes is considerably less vivid than the other because it is made by the part of the sun that is partly obstructed by the rather dirty window. How difficult would it be to clean that window? Almost certainly not too difficult at all, and almost certainly worth the effort. To be able to see things as they actually are. A day like today may never happen again, and here's our protagonist, sitting at his desk. The musician outside is not a classical guitarist, actually, but a ragtime piano player. That feels more fitting.

Now outside—unshackled from his desk, self-liberated from his rented walls—our protagonist applauds the woman who plays the upright piano, which is on wheels, which are on the sidewalk. Possibly he would give her a small amount of money if he had some money with him, but he didn't bring any money with him because he didn't want to spend any money. But he really likes this ragtime piano music. Easily enough, he knows, he could run back up to his apartment and grab some coins for the ragtime piano player; it would take less than one minute. It would be so easy.

He walks, with no plan, through the town and out of the town and off the main road and onto a narrow path between trees. What kind of trees? Tall trees. What more needs to be known? The sky is changing fast, and that is more important to know about than the trees. Why? Because now it is raining. The sun-filled air has been replaced with water-filled air. If our protagonist had anticipated this, maybe he would have brought his umbrella with him or maybe he wouldn't have come outside at all or maybe nothing would be any different from the way it is now. Since it's impossible to know if he would have done anything differently if he had known, one hour ago, what now would be like, speculating seems kind of stupid.

Anyhow, he's out here now, in rain that could not be accurately described as gentle, and he knows, as he has for as long as he can remember, there is nothing he can do to make rain go away. This weather's fine, he tells himself—maybe because he knows it's better to tell himself that than the opposite thing, and maybe not too much harder. Maybe it isn't even harder at all.

The sea is fairly close now, but still can't be seen. Even though he is getting very wet and cold, he doesn't turn around to return to town because he likes to look at the sea and wants to look at it again. As he continues to walk down the narrow path between tall trees he stops paying attention to what's around him and starts to imagine, imagining that, in a few minutes, he will be standing on the cliff, on the edge of the land, and looking at the sea, and there will be no horizon: the sea will meet the sky at some unknown place: it will be impossible to tell where one thing ends and the other thing begins—so, in a way, there will no longer be any difference between the things. Is that how it will be?

A few minutes later he is out of the trees and standing on the cliff, on the edge of the land, and looking at the sea, and this actual view is essentially identical to his minutes-ago imagination: there is no horizon: the sky and the sea are the same incomprehensibly big thing, which is simultaneously infinitesimal. Water is everywhere—below, to the sides, above—and somehow the wetness of this rock—this cliff on which he stands— makes it seem more real than reality.

Instead of turning around to return to town— which would really be the sensible thing to do, considering that his clothes are soaked and he is very cold—he begins to walk along the edge of the cliff, and he keeps walking along the edge of the cliff until a mighty gust of wind blows him off the cliff.

As our protagonist falls, through the water-filled air, he berates himself for walking so close to the edge of the cliff. How stupid! This is quite a fall, and it may very well cause death.

Floating on his back in the sea, he is surprised by how similar his current position feels to his former position. Probably because he had already gotten thoroughly soaked by rain. With seawater in his ears, he observes the cliff on which he so recently stood. How quickly things can change! And suddenly he feels absurdly lucky to be alive. Yes, the waters of today have made him very cold, but he is very happy he decided to come outside, into the world, this afternoon; if he hadn't gotten blown off a cliff, he probably wouldn't have experienced a gratitude for life that is even remotely comparable to the gratitude for life that he is experiencing right now.

Imagining ragtime piano music—because he can and because, somehow, that music makes him feel a little warmer—he begins to swim toward the land.

Going and Going

The sun is now hiding behind the trees on the western edge of the dog park. Honey looks at his watch—5:04. *Summer was just here*, he thinks, *and suddenly it's long gone*. He chuckles.

"What's so funny now?" says his wife, Laura, not turning to look at him but keeping her eyes on their dog, Pickle, who just dropped the ball for the third time on his way back. Apparently realizing that the ball is gone again, Pickle stops and turns around—but, instead of moving to retrieve the ball again, he lies down on the grass.

"Time!" says Honey, chuckling again.

"Time is funny?"

"It just keeps going and going! Good luck trying to stop it!"

An airplane, tens of thousands of feet above their heads, is drawing a line on the orange sky.

Though Laura is moderately disturbed by the fast passage of time—they are both well into middle age, and too often she feels like she already has one foot in the grave—she appreciates Honey's good humor. When, many years ago, she told her mother and her father and her younger sister about her engagement to Honey, none of them was very supportive of the match. They disapproved of Honey because they thought he didn't take things seriously enough, that he somehow viewed almost everything in life as some kind of joke. The thing is, they were pretty much correct: Honey did, and does, lack anything resembling seriousness. But his lack of seriousness has always been one of the main reasons why Laura likes him so much.

Pickle is still lying on the grass. "He's not going to come back, is he?" says Laura.

Honey laughs. "No way. And I respect that. He used to do everything we expected him to do, but he has clearly decided that now, as he enters his more mature years, he's going to do things on his own terms."

"Or, in this case, do nothing on his own terms."

Honey laughs. "Nothing is still something."

"Maybe…"

Honey laughs. "Yes, maybe it isn't. How should I know?" He tilts his head back, slightly, and says, quite loudly in Pickle's direction, and with a big smile on his face, "Get over here you mangy mutt!"

Pickle lifts his head, swivels it, and looks at Honey and Laura—but, instead of getting back up on his paws, he returns his head to its former position on the grass.

"He probably doesn't appreciate being called a mangy mutt," says Laura.

"I meant it as a term of affection."

Without another word, and in unison, Laura and Honey start to cross the distance to Pickle. The airplane is no longer visible from here and the line it drew is slowly disappearing. Upon reaching Pickle, Honey crouches and pats the dog on the head a few times.

As they walk on a path through the trees, toward the city streets and their apartment, pieces of the low red sun occasionally sneak through the branches. The sounds are their steps, faint barks from the dog park behind them, and orange and red and yellow leaves coming into contact with the earth, assisted by light wind.

"I guess it's really autumn," says Laura.

"After all this time, time is still going and going!" Honey laughs. "It just won't give up!"

"Bob Dylan has a line… 'Time is a jet plane; it moves too fast.'"

"Time is a jet plane…" says Honey, with a thoughtful expression on his face. And then, after a few moments, he laughs yet again.

The First Café I Encountered

One clear Saturday morning I left my place with no destination in mind. I walked through suburban streets and then woods and then more suburban streets, and eventually I found myself in a nice little town. Feeling quite hungry, I entered the first café I encountered.

As soon as I brought a piece of quiche and a cup of coffee to a table next to a window, I stopped feeling hungry. I looked at the little plant in the little pot that was placed in the center of my table and thought about the woods I had walked through to get here. The woods had been very peaceful, with the branches above and the branches to the sides moving slightly in the slight wind, with sunlight breaking through the dense foliage, fleetingly, quite a few times per second, with the sound of water, somewhere then unclear, running over rocks.

A man moves a chair away from the next table, goes away, then returns, wheeling over a wheelchair to occupy the vacant spot. The wheelchair is occupied by a very old man whose head is tilted to the left. The man who wheeled over the wheelchair is not young himself—he must be at least fifty years old—and he now sits on the opposite side of the table—he and the very old man are now facing each other—and he now reaches into a satchel and pulls out two copies of the local newspaper and carefully places one directly in front of the very old man and the other one directly in front of himself, and now the woman at the counter calls out a name I don't catch, and now the man rises, walks to the counter, then returns to his table with two cups of coffee and carefully places one directly in front of the very old man and the other one directly in front of his own seat, and now he returns to the counter, then returns to his table holding two plates, each of which holds a croissant, and carefully places one directly in front of the very old man and the other one directly in front of his own seat, and now he finally sits again.

Aside from the slight movements caused by breathing, the very old man has not moved at all.

Suddenly I find myself thinking about the woods again. For quite a long time I could hear water without being able to see any water. Eventually I got so frustrated that I left the path and made my way downhill, navigating branches, until I finally reached a creek. Insects were flitting across the surface. After skipping a few thin stones I crossed the creek, taking careful steps on the stones that were too large to be covered by the gently running water.

The younger-but-not-young man transfers his attention from his copy of the local newspaper to the very old man—who still hasn't looked at his copy of the local newspaper, who still hasn't taken a sip of his coffee, who still hasn't taken a bite of his croissant—and asks if he needs any help. With a smile the very old man reaches out—slowly—grabs and lifts his croissant—slowly—takes a small bite of croissant and chews—slowly—and swallows. The angle of his head still hasn't changed, is still tilted to the left in exactly the same way. The very old man returns his croissant to his plate, and the younger-but-not-young man returns his attention to his copy of the local newspaper.

Finally I begin to eat my own food. The quiche is very good. Looking out the window as I chew, I see a woman ride by on a blue bicycle.

When I look at the very old man again his head is tilted more to the left than before—and, as moments and more moments pass, it seems like he is no longer breathing. "Excuse me," I say to the younger-but-not-young man, who, in response to my words, transfers his attention from the local newspaper to me, "but is he OK?"

As he looks over at the very old man, as he pushes his chair back and stands and reaches out a hand to investigate, I find myself thinking that if this very old man has, indeed, died, there are many, many worse ways to do so.

Horizontal Raindrop

Every day, after school, Leo goes to the library. Just beyond the entrance, on the left, there's a pretty big fish tank.

Five fishes live in the tank.

Three are sleek silver with a few bright crisp yellow lines. These three seem to think very highly of themselves.

One is quite dark and very shy. This one hides by the bottom, behind fake coral.

And one always has a big smile on his face. And this one *always*, as soon as Leo walks over, swims over to Leo's face and smiles at him through the glass—clearly saying hello. This one is a muddy light grey, and his body thins out from his wide face to his tail: he looks like a horizontal raindrop.

There are some spiky things on his sides, but they don't seem aggressive or unpleasant. They look like soft spikes.

Almost everyone, Leo has noticed, walks right past the fish tank without stopping to look. Leo does not understand how they do that. Because Leo always stops to look. And he loves it when his fish friend—the horizontal raindrop with the big smile and the soft spikes—rushes over to say hello. This is always one of the best parts of Leo's day.

This morning Leo had a math test. He feels like he didn't do nearly as well as he could have. He is disappointed with himself.

And so, as he enters the library today, he is really, really looking forward to his fish friend's warm greeting. He senses that his fish friend will cheer him up.

He walks over to the tank and looks through the glass.

His fish friend does not swim over.

After looking through the glass from as many different angles as possible, Leo concludes that his fish friend is not in the tank.

Where is he?

With a bad feeling in his stomach, Leo walks away from the tank and sits at a table and begins his homework. But he finds it very difficult to focus on anything other than his absent fish friend. Where could he be? The most likely explanation, Leo supposes, is that his fish friend is dead. But… Well, he always looked like he was in the prime of his life! He certainly never looked like a fish on his last fins.

An old woman at the next table has extremely tanned and extremely shriveled skin. Leo looks away. His fish friend certainly wasn't in her kind of condition.

Maybe he was just taken away for a little while. The library has some programs for kids (due to shyness, Leo has not participated in any of them), and maybe sometimes a kid is allowed to take a fish home for a few days.

Another possibility: one of the librarians noticed some minor issue with his fish friend's health and took him to a fish doctor.

Another possiblity: a wealthy library patron bought his fish friend and took him to live in an even more luxurious fish tank.

There are, Leo assures himself, many plausible explanations for the absence.

With a not-quite-as-bad feeling in his stomach, Leo begins to focus on his homework.

The next afternoon Leo reaches the library door, reaches out to push it open—and turns around and goes home.

The next afternoon Leo manages to cross the threshold. Somewhat hesitantly, he walks over to the tank and looks through the glass.

Those three sleek silver fish, with their bright crisp yellow lines, are still there, still parading themselves around.

The dark shy fish is still hiding behind the fake coral.

And Leo's fish friend is still absent.

Where is he?

With a bad feeling in his stomach, Leo walks away from the tank and sits at a table and does not begin his homework. Instead, he considers his options.

He could ask one of the librarians about his fish friend. Surely one of them knows what happened to him. The problem with that option, though, is that Leo is very concerned about what he might learn.

So he decides to select what may be his only other option: to never ask about what happened to his fish friend. Leo prefers this option because it will allow him to at least *hope* that his fish friend is still moving around somewhere in the world, alive and well.

Leo walks back over to the tank and looks through the glass.

Everything is the same as it was before. No fish friend.

Leo sighs.

But then, just as he is about to turn around and walk away, something completely unexpected happens:

the dark shy fish emerges from behind the fake coral and swims up to Leo's face.

As they look at each other through the glass, Leo feels certain that the dark shy fish is finally saying hello.

Summer Reading

Julia is back home for the summer, having just completed her first year of college, and she in absolutely no way views this summer break as an actual break. In addition to having a demanding internship she is independently continuing her studies of psychology. At the end of the semester she met with several of her professors, asked for reading recommendations, and compiled a list. Thirty-two books are on her list, and she intends to read all of them by the beginning of the fall semester. She has now been back home for a little over a week and, thanks to a highly structured morning and evening reading schedule, has already completed three substantial books.

But Julia is also setting aside a little bit of time each week to visit with friends from high school—because a number of psychological studies have demonstrated the positive effects of long-term friendships.

Unfortunately, the old friend Julia had planned to meet tonight just called and informed her that, due to something unexpected, they actually would not be able to meet tonight.

So Julia now has an open evening.

On the long bus ride home from her internship she makes decent progress on one of her psychology books, occasionally making notes in a spiral-bound notebook.

At the dinner table her parents say it's too bad her plans got cancelled, and then ask if she wants to watch a movie with them and her little brother after dinner.

Julia says she should work on her studies.

"You know, it could be nice to relax a little," says her father. "It's good to do something different once in a while."

Julia says she should work on her studies. And then, after a pause, she continues: "But I *do* agree with you about the importance of variety. Which is why, tonight, I'll study in the backyard."

This really is a perfect evening for studying outside, Julia notes to herself shortly after sitting on some grass not far from the creek behind the house. The air is soothing and the evening light is soothing and the water sounds are soothing.

And now she directs her attention at the words on page 78 of the book in her hands. The words are moderately interesting… But the font is so small!

By the time Julia reaches page 81 she feels like she is starting to get a headache.

The book is closed and placed to the side, on grass.

Julia gets up and walks as close to the water as she can without touching the water, and looks down.

A little fish swims by.

Many trees are around, and a light summer wind is moving the leaves of the trees and even—though almost imperceptibly—some of the branches of the trees.

The sun is now quite close to the land.

Turning around, Julia notices movement above the gentle slope and through the big living room window: the TV is on. Julia begins to move up the gentle slope, in order to investigate the moving images.

When she is close enough to recognize Venice, she stops. After a few moments she remembers that she saw this movie years ago, remembers the name of this movie, remembers that she had enjoyed this movie.

As Julia watches the main character move around Venice, she almost wishes she had made a different decision, almost wishes she had agreed to take a break from her studies and watch a movie with her family. But she assures herself that she doesn't actually regret her decision—because she has important studying to do.

Standing there on the grass, watching the moving images on the TV screen on the other side of the big living room window, Julia wonders if she will ever make it to Venice.

She certainly hopes that she will.

The Most Important Thing

I like to play chess. I like the fact that when you lose a game you can't blame anyone other than yourself. Because you don't have any teammates, and absolutely no luck is involved.

Every once in a while an old friend from college and I get together for a lunch followed by a game of chess. It's a nice tradition. Usually we play on his little balcony.

His little balcony is on the third floor of his apartment building, and his apartment building is right next to a nice park, and the nice park has some very tall, very robust trees. When we're out there, on his little balcony, it kind of feels like we're in a treehouse, since we're pretty high up and those tall, robust trees are right next to us. I mean, we can almost touch the branches!

Anyhow, last Saturday I took the bus over to his neighborhood. After we ate some tacos in the park, we went up to his balcony for our chess match. Historically I have probably won 75% of our matches, so I felt pretty confident that I would win again (and even if I had only won 25% of our matches I, in all likelihood, would still have thought I would win: I am pretty competitive, and pretty much whenever I enter any competition I feel pretty confident that I'll find a way to win).

But, on the balcony last Saturday, I did not win. It was a long game, and though I definitely had the advantage for a while, I lost.

Then he brought a speaker out to the balcony and we listened to music and talked about music and other things. The wind picked up and moved the branches around a bit, but it was still quite warm and pleasant out there, on the balcony. At one point a squirrel arrived and ran along some branches.

Then my friend's girlfriend came out to the balcony. I hadn't yet seen her that day—she had been doing something somewhere else, I don't know what or where. "Did you play your game?"

My friend nodded his head slowly. "Yes."

"And who won today?"

My friend looked at me. "It really doesn't matter who won," I said. "The most important thing is that we both had a lot of fun."

"Ah," she said. I think she knew I hated to admit defeat, and that lying—saying that having fun was the most important thing—was the easiest way for me to indicate that I had, indeed, lost the game.

We kept listening to music. We drank some coffee. The colors of the pieces of sky I could see through the branches were changing. The evening was announcing itself. I left.

On the bus ride back home I ran into someone we'd gone to college with. I hadn't seen her in years. We got to talking, and I mentioned whom I'd spent the afternoon with.

"How's he doing?"

"He's doing just fine," I said.

"How did you guys spend the afternoon?"

"Tacos and chess."

"Who won?"

Why, I wondered, would she ask that question? I hadn't seen her in years, and suddenly she was pretending to care about who won our game?

"You know," I said, "it really doesn't matter who won. The most important thing is that we both had a lot of fun."

In that moment, the strangest thing happened: as I heard myself saying those words I realized, amazingly, that I actually almost believed them.

Castro Theatre

The organist on the stage is performing music from "Lawrence of Arabia." The film that will soon begin is, unsurprisingly, "Lawrence of Arabia." The favorite film of several people in attendance tonight is, unsurprisingly, "Lawrence of Arabia."

They don't make movies like "Lawrence of Arabia" anymore, says one audience member to another.

This is a Grand Old Movie Palace. The massive Art Deco chandelier proves that this is, undoubtedly, a Grand Old Movie Palace. The devoted organist, who comes here night after night after night, who learns the musical themes of film after film after film—including the musical themes of films he doesn't even like—further proves that this is, undoubtedly, a Grand Old Movie Palace.

They don't make Grand Old Movie Palaces like this anymore, says one audience member to another.

And now, up on the stage, there is vertical movement: the mechanized descent of the organ and the organist is underway. The intensity of the music increases: this is the finale of the pre-film concert.

And now the finale of the pre-film concert is over. The audience applauds.

And now the curtain moves and the lights go down. The film is about to begin.

Napoleon Dictating His Reminiscences

It must be said: Elba was way better. They still called me Emperor there! Sure, there weren't even 15,000 people on the island, so it wasn't exactly a *remarkable* territory to rule... But at least I *could* rule.

And I developed some pretty significant projects there.

But here, on this godforsaken little rock, almost nobody respects me. Yes, it's comforting to know that in the souls of millions and millions of Europeans I am still Emperor... But here, on St. Helena, almost everybody—aside from my few remaining disciples—calls me, all too mundanely, Napoleon. It's a real drag.

And then there's my "Custodian." The dreadful—*dreadful!*—Hudson Lowe. How he condescends to me! But he's nothing more than yet another tiny governor. And, though Lowe has not provided even the slightest indication of a functional mind, I think it quite likely that he understands, or at least intuitively senses, the fact that the sole reason his existence has *any* historical value is because I, The Emperor, happened to be deposited into his tiny sphere of influence.

If I have learned anything during my stay on this planet, it is that the worst things happen to the best people. If you doubt that statement, just look at Julius Caesar. Then look at me.

Two geniuses unjustly derailed from their proper trajectories.

And now I'm stuck in the deplorable Longwood House.

Longwood House is very cold.

Longwood House is bursting with rats.

Longwood House seems on the verge of collapse.

This is no place for The Emperor!

The people of Elba were sad when I left. I don't blame them. In my brief time on their island I made many improvements; when I left it was a much more ordered, civilized place than it was when I arrived. In all likelihood, they'll have an annual parade in my honor. For centuries! Probably there are already at least a few statues of their dear Emperor scattered around the island.

I probably should have stayed on Elba. I didn't appreciate the place as much as I should have. One can never fully appreciate what one has until it's gone.

But, really, when it comes to leaving Elba, I had no choice: when a man knows he has a unique ability to enact sweeping, positive change, he has a responsibility—not only to himself, but to mankind as well—to take action. Yes, I really had no choice: I had to try to take over Europe again. I owed mankind that much.

So here I am, stuck in a cold run-down house on a godforsaken little rock. While dictating this little account to Jacques, I have seen at least a dozen rats scurrying around. Though I have annihilated countless vermin during my stay here, more always arrive. So now I don't even bother with annihilation.

This is not a nice place.

But... to be perfectly honest... increasingly often I feel like I myself am not too dissimilar to those rats.

Jacques, please delete that last line. It makes me sound too pitiful. Wait—are you dictating what I'm saying now?

So... *how* did I end up here?

Oh, yes. I tried to do something grand... And I failed.

I was convinced I would succeed... But I failed.

But, you know, at least I tried.

And, you know, there *is* something impressive about having been exiled twice. My knowledge of history is, as everybody knows, extensive, and I am unable to think of anybody else who has been exiled twice.

And one can't be exiled if one doesn't attempt something grand. People who never risk anything never get exiled.

Alright, Jacques, that's enough for now. We'll continue tomorrow.

Oh—before you leave, let me share some good news: I might have figured out a way to get off this damn island!

On Green Terraces

The sleek surfaces and mechanical exclamations of the city are gone, and now I am rambling around on green terraces. Though these green terraces might have a deliberate order, they appear—kind of charmingly—disordered. Stones make up the walls and the steps from one terrace to the next, and as I wander I wonder how many generations have come and gone since these stones were placed. Trees, arranged throughout in a way that seems unarranged, gently distribute shadows. As the sun is not at all bashful today, more than half of the people in this big irregular park have positioned themselves in shade. This is a day that can almost see the summer.

Now, when immersed in undeniable pleasantness, is as good a time as any to again remember and regret all of the major decisions made thus far, in this particular life. What exactly *were* those thought processes? How could I have been so stupid?

Sufficient explanations are not presenting themselves.

Meanwhile these people around me, in this big irregular park, in the sunshine and in the shade, are… It seems as though not one of them has a single problem. Everything is wonderful for all of these people. They have all figured out exactly how to live, and they are all proceeding with admirable conviction. Many are sitting or lying on grass or on benches, and quite a few are walking or running or standing almost still or stretching, and some are in small groups and some are alone, and some are talking and some are reading and some are writing and some are playing music—and all appear content. No doubt is evident. They are all absolutely thrilled with life.

Having moved over so many of these green terraces—situated up and down multiple slopes, converging and diverging in unexpected ways, forming many different shapes with all sorts of unexpected angles—I no longer know where I am in relation to where I entered this big irregular park, and from my current position no clear exit is visible. The farthest walls I can see are uninterrupted stones. Where is an opening that will allow me to get back into the city? Maybe I wouldn't be so lost right now if I hadn't been so focused on how I possibly ruined my life—but that had seemed like an important thing to think about, like something that warranted scrutiny. In any case, now I really have to get back into the city as quickly as possible, as I really need to figure out how to turn things around, how to become a big success before I run out of time.

A well-dressed young woman is curled on a bench, seemingly sleeping, with a book for a pillow and an unzipped backpack on the grass. How can she be comfortable in such a position, with a book for a pillow? How can she disregard the possibility that someone could easily attack her? How can she trust that nobody will steal her backpack while her consciousness is elsewhere? It's baffling, what she's doing, sleeping in public like that, letting herself be so vulnerable.

Reaching what I suspect is one of the edges of this place, I am facing a high wall of stones with no opening. To get out of here I will have to take stone steps to a different terrace, but I do not know whether going down or going up will get me out of here faster. Though this big irregular park certainly has charm, and though this is certainly—at least in theory—a perfect day to be here, I have so many serious things to accomplish today, and must...

I decide to ascend, and find myself on a large semicircular terrace where an old man is lying on grass, seemingly sleeping, in the shade of a tree. There is no exit here either, so I go up to the next terrace, which is almost a rhombus, and see a middle-aged couple lying on a blanket in the sunshine, arms around each other, also seemingly sleeping. There is no exit here either, so I go up to the next terrace, which is almost an isosceles triangle. There is no exit here either—but why am I so desperate to leave? Yes, I have some very serious things to accomplish... But this really could be a perfect day. Other people have found a way to be comfortable here— so shouldn't I be able to find a way to be comfortable here?

I sit on grass and lean against a wall of stones. Two people stop running not too far away and start stretching and, though they look like they are enjoying each other's company, complain about something or other—it is not clear, from this distance, what. As they run off, down stone steps to the rhombus terrace, I realize what really should have been obvious all along: all of the people in this big irregular park have their own problems. Not everything is perfect for everyone else. It can just seem that way sometimes because personal travails and doubts usually aren't on the surface and obvious; they are not like mountains, but oxygen. But at least all of these people made it here, to these wonderful green terraces, to this possibly perfect day. And it's pretty amazing that I'm here too.

I put my head on grass and close my eyes and begin to dream about a big irregular park in which everyone has decided to stop paying attention to time.

Thin Cardigan

Friends are visiting.

A few weeks ago Alice spontaneously invited John and Nicole to come out here for a few days and, somewhat to her surprise, they booked flights almost immediately.

So here they are.

Some of the things they ask Alice indicate concern.

"Are you doing OK out here?" says Nicole.

Though the transition to her new life out here has not exactly been easy, Alice says "Yes, I'm doing very well."

"Have you met many people?" says John.

"Yes."

"It could be nice to meet some of your new friends."

Alice doesn't know what to say. Because she hasn't managed to develop, over the course of her six months out here, anything she would feel comfortable calling a friendship. Yes, she has fine relationships with her colleagues at work, but…

For a few weeks now she has been wondering if it was a mistake to move out here. Yes, she has a pretty good job, but…

Anyhow, she really appreciates that John and Nicole have come out here to visit her, and she decides to do her best to make their days out here as enjoyable as possible.

They just had dinner at a nice little restaurant, and now they are sitting on Alice's nice little balcony. There are no clouds, and the stars are much brighter out here than they are back in the big city.

For quite a while they've been reminiscing about old times. Though Alice had been enjoying this, she suddenly feels nauseous; life is very short, and here they are wasting the present by talking about the past.

So she abruptly changes the subject by asking what they should all do tomorrow. John and Nicole don't know too much about this area—they have never been out here before—so Alice gives the matter some thought, and then proposes some activities. A discussion of the various options concludes with the decision to do something Alice has heard about but never done: take the aerial tram from the desert floor to the top of the mountain.

The aerial tram lifts them into the clear morning sky. About forty people are occupying this space.

Some people are having quiet conversations.

Some people are silent.

Some of the talking people and some of the silent people are looking through the windows at the changing view.

Some of the talking people and some of the silent people are looking at their cell phones.

Alice and John and Nicole are talking about some of the recent changes in the big city that Alice, until recently, called home, and Alice is listening and asking some decent questions, but she is simultaneously focusing on the changing view on the other side of the windows.

Sand has already been replaced by boulders and cliffs. Since there is not much vegetation, this part of the mountain looks severe, uncompromising. *Not conducive to life*, thinks Alice, *because there simply…*

"What's that?" says Alice, realizing that she has just been asked a question and that she has absolutely no idea what the question is. Nicole asks the question again. "Oh, yes," says Alice, "they actually changed that before I moved away."

The aerial tram is ascending quite quickly—and so, only a few minutes later, big trees begin to materialize on the mountainside, along with an increasingly wide array of other plants. Alice enjoys watching the view get greener and greener.

And now the view begins to turn white. Though Alice remembers seeing snow in the distance, from the base of the mountain, it is still a bit jarring to see it up close, after being surrounded by sand and heat and more sand for so long. She brought along a thin cardigan, and she now suspects that she should have brought along something more substantial than a thin cardigan. Oh well.

And now they are walking along a path, on snow, and there are big trees all around. They can see their breath.

This cold, cold air makes Alice feel extremely awake. She's glad she didn't bring a warmer layer.

The path turns sharply, and soon Alice and John and Nicole are standing on the edge of the mountain, with a clear view of the desert and scattered towns far, far below. Everything down there looks infinitesimal. Everything down there *is* infinitesimal. This is a good perspective. And perspective is so important.

Sure, maybe things haven't worked out as easily as Alice had thought they would; maybe she has, recently, been more alone than she would like. So she decides, right now, to do more, to work harder to meet new people. And eventually, she believes, something good will happen.

In any case, this particular day is very, very beautiful.

"Where exactly do you live?" says John.

Alice studies the desert and scattered towns for a few moments—and suddenly she feels almost unbelievably happy. Because, even though she can't clearly see the structure itself, she knows exactly where she lives.

"There," she says, extending her right arm and pointing with her right index finger. "I live right there." And then she says, after lowering her arm and turning toward John and Nicole, "Thanks again for visiting me out here. I'm really glad you came."

Look Out! The Future!

It is not late but it is already dark. This is that time of year. As Leo turns the corner he instinctively examines the bus stop and surrounding area. Nobody is there. As he approaches the bus stop he examines the street. No bus is out there. He puts his backpack on the sidewalk, next to bench, and puts his left foot on the bench, which makes him feel—though he does not articulate the feeling—like he belongs here.

Today there had been quite a few things to do at school, and, as usual, Leo did what he had to do. But only one thing made a real impression on him today, and that one thing was something he overheard a classmate say in the hallway: "I want to be a dentist."

What Leo finds so impressive—amazing, really— is the conviction with which Michelle said those words. There is no doubt in Leo's mind that Michelle really, really wants to be a dentist. *But how*, thinks Leo, *does she know that? And… am I supposed to know what I want to be?* His consciousness tightens, quite unpleasantly. *In less than three years I'll be in high school! I need to start figuring out my career.*

He stands on the bench and begins to think about what he should do with his life. It is difficult for him to see the appeal of a career in dentistry.

What is the most logical way to figure out what to be? How to fill the hours and days and months and years and decades (if lucky) that are life?

Hopping off the bench and unzipping his backpack, he takes out his books and carefully places them on the sidewalk—trying to make them as parallel and evenly spaced as possible—and looks at one book, then another, then another, then another; and now he stands on the bench again and looks at the books from up there, sensing that the extra height could somehow be helpful.

Which subject seems most interesting?

What we've been learning about in science class, thinks Leo, *has been kind of cool. Maybe you could work in a cool lab. Or be a veterinarian. You like animals…*

Taking a few slow steps on the bench, Leo examines the street. No bus is out there.

And now he is looking at the bus stop's big map of the city and the various bus routes. He knows where he is right now and where he is going and what some of the stuff in between looks like, but most of the places represented on the big map remain unknown. There is a lot—out there, all around—to discover.

Leo waves at the bus as he runs over to the part of the sidewalk where his books are neatly arranged. The bus stops just as Leo puts the last book in his backpack. The door opens. Leo climbs the steps and shows the bus driver, whom he recognizes, his pass, and the bus driver nods.

About half of the seats are occupied. With the words "I want to be a dentist" still in his head, Leo inspects—surreptitiously, he hopes—the other passengers. While he is able to infer that the woman who wears a nun's habit is a nun, he is unable to reasonably infer what any of the others do for a living.

Startlingly, he realizes he only recognizes three of the people here (well, four if you count the bus driver); this startles him because he rides this bus at this time pretty much every weekday, and he would expect there to be more people like him, more people who ride this bus at this time pretty much every weekday. Instead, he is surrounded by unfamiliar faces; *and you will probably*, he thinks, *never see most of these faces again*. And at this time tomorrow he will, in all likelihood, be surrounded by a roughly equal number of unfamiliar faces; *and you will probably*, he thinks, *never see most of those faces again, either*. There are so many people in this city! In this world! *And almost everyone you see over the course of your life*, he thinks, *you will see one time and never again*.

As he reaches into his backpack to take out his science textbook to prepare for his career—this is a thirty-five-minute bus ride, so he has time—he notices the novel he checked out yesterday. Suddenly it's the 1700s and two brothers are flying around Europe on an airship (a sailing ship that, thanks to a system of copper spheres and a vacuum pump, actually flies) invented by one of the brothers, and even though it really seems like this airship really was flying around Europe in the 1700s (several important historical figures appear and make the whole story seem quite authentic), Leo is fairly certain that no such airship actually existed in the 1700s. But that doesn't matter to him, because he thoroughly enjoys reading about these sky-sailing brothers and their travels. And now they are on their way to the North Pole! The airship rises, the sails are adjusted, and more of the world is about to—

"Hey! Kid! Hey! Kid! Hey!" says the bus driver—who, Leo sees, is looking at him. "Isn't this where you usually get off?"

Leo sees a fragment of his neighborhood on the other side of the window. "Yes, this is where I get off."

The bus driver chuckles. "That must be a pretty good book."

"Yes, it is a pretty good book." Leo goes down a step—then stops and turns around. "Bye."

"Have a good one," says the bus driver, and Leo gets onto the sidewalk, and the bus goes away.

Leo likes that bus driver. That bus driver always seems to be in a pretty good mood. Maybe it's fun to be a bus driver. Then again, maybe it isn't. *Maybe one day*, thinks Leo, *you should ask that bus driver if he likes being a bus driver*.

Though Leo still doesn't know what he wants to be, he does know at least one thing: he would rather be a bus driver than a dentist.

Foreign Land

And now the traveler arrives in the foreign land where, for a number of days, he will be on his own.

After making his way to his lodging, putting his bag in his room, and quickly washing up, he goes out into the street and, with no destination in mind, arbitrarily decides to go left.

The sun, low in the sky, fills the hazy air with slanted golden light that gives the whole scene—with all those people moving along the sidewalks and all those vehicles moving along the streets and all those buildings all around—a nostalgic quality, as though everything that one would initially assume is happening right now actually happened long ago.

As though the present were a memory.

And that slanted-golden-light scene in the bustling capital soon enough actually *is* a memory: after a brief stay in the bustling capital the traveler traveled to a different part of this foreign land, and now he is walking through a very large and very old garden.

This very large and very old garden has many different sections. Some sections are extremely ordered.

Some sections appear to have been allowed to grow without the interventions of gardeners.

The traveler sits next to a pond and looks at the reflections of plants and clouds on the water.

As the traveler walks along the river—from the garden to the main part of the town—he sees a man and a woman sitting on a bench, a group of uniformed schoolchildren riding by on bicycles, and a big shaggy dog sleeping in the shade of a big shaggy tree.

And now, in yet another lodging, the traveler is eating a simple breakfast and talking with a man who has spent quite a bit of time, he says, in prison. He had been a thief, he says, and he sounds oddly proud when recounting his thefts before finally getting caught. If he had blindly followed the values on which he was raised he would not, he says, have become a thief, would not have ended up in prison. But, instead, his life has turned out to be unconventional and interesting because, he says, he is fearless and creative.

Though the traveler does not quite know how he feels about the former prisoner and his tale, it is with a feeling of some relief that he exits the lodging, all on his own again, to do exactly as he pleases.

Moving under a bright white sky, the traveler tries to appreciate the architecture. And, to a certain extent, he does. But the thing is… The thing is that while it is nice to be all on his own so he can do exactly as he pleases… Well, the traveler supposes that, in a way, it actually *had* been nice to talk with the former prisoner, because… Well, because the traveler has had too few conversations since arriving in this foreign land.

Yes: it can be very nice to talk with someone even if you don't necessarily agree with what that someone is saying.

The traveler realizes that the pleasant solitude of traveling alone has been replaced by loneliness.

Thank God today is Wednesday! Because tomorrow the traveler will… Well, if the plan actually works…

The traveler has learned, many times, that plans really aren't reliable.

Trying to disregard his trepidation, the traveler returns to the capital on Thursday, makes his way to the agreed-upon meeting place, and…

There! The traveler's friend is there!

How could the traveler have experienced such doubt? Of course the plan worked!

Smiles are exchanged.

The traveler is happy. Because, while there are certainly good things about traveling alone, it is usually better to travel with another.

Unexpected Paradise

Some ducks migrate. Some ducks don't migrate. But even the ducks that don't migrate usually go on at least a few short trips throughout the year. The general thinking, among ducks, is that it's healthy to get a change of scenery once in a while.

By now it's probably obvious that the main characters of this story are ducks. Two ducks. One duck has a spotless beak and the other duck has a beak with an unusual spot on it. The first duck is known as Clean Beak and the second duck is known as Beak With Spot.

By now it's probably obvious that most ducks are not very good at coming up with good names.

Clean Beak and Beak With Spot have just found a nice new place to stay. The water smells a bit odd… But it's still nice to float on. And since the water is surrounded by some kind of human construction, they are protected from the wind. Though the ducks don't care for the human construction itself—in terms of aesthetics—today is very windy, so they certainly appreciate the protection it provides.

So here they are, Clean Beak and Beak With Spot, sometimes enjoying the pool, sometimes enjoying the concrete around the pool—either lounging around or waddling around.

Once in a while they notice a human or multiple humans moving around in the distance—walking up some stairs or walking down some stairs, opening a door or closing a door—but the ducks have the whole pool area to themselves.

Well, they do…

Until they don't.

Suddenly a man is very close to the pool. Clean Beak and Beak With Spot get nervous. They remain on the water, but are prepared to flee in an instant. The man places a big thing on the water. The big thing floats.

The man gets onto the big floating thing.

Clean Beak and Beak With Spot are still nervous. But, though the man has clearly noticed them, he seems content to leave them to their own devices. As time passes, the ducks gradually get less nervous. And eventually they think it's kind of nice to share this space with someone else.

After the man and the sun have gone away, Clean Beak and Beak With Spot are relaxing on the concrete, getting quite drowsy…

An unexpected light bursts into being.

The ducks hop up, frightened. As their eyes adjust, a woman comes into focus.

The woman is right next to the bright light. She is in a part of this place that the ducks do not like—the part of this place where the water is way too hot.

The bright light is directed at something the woman is holding in her hands. Something that seems to absorb all of her attention. The ducks realize that the hot water woman does not intend to hurt them. Maybe she hasn't even noticed them.

Clean Beak expresses, in the manner in which ducks share thoughts with one another, his belief that there is something very, very special about the hot water woman's bright light.

Beak With Spot expresses, with the frankness for which ducks are known, his opinion, which is that it was much more pleasant out here before the obtrusion of the hot water woman's bright light.

Each duck thinks the other duck is completely wrong.

They abandon the subject. They are fairly certain that their respective opinions will not change, which means that any kind of debate will, in all likelihood, only lead to ruffled feathers.

Clean Beak, transfixed, does not look away from the bright light.

Beak With Spot has turned around to look in the opposite direction.

The next day Clean Beak and Beak With Spot notice, in the distance, the man with whom they shared the pool. He is moving toward the pool. This time, though, he doesn't have the big floating thing with him. This time he's holding a loaf of bread.

Clean Beak and Beak With Spot know all about bread. Every once in a while they encounter a friendly human who seems to enjoy tossing little pieces of bread in their direction. Getting little pieces of bread tossed in their direction is—and this is a point on which Clean Beak and Beak With Spot are in full agreement—a wonderful thing.

A wonderful thing that does not happen nearly as often as they would like.

Are they going to get little pieces of bread tossed in their direction now? They know they shouldn't get their hopes up, since the man could be planning to enjoy the bread himself.

Floating there, Clean Beak and Beak With Spot watch the man get closer, and closer, and closer. They are really trying to not get their hopes up.

And now he's standing on the edge of the pool…

And now he's tearing off a little piece of bread…

And now he's tossing the little piece of bread in their direction!

Clean Beak and Beak With Spot are moving fast before the bread hits the water.

When the man has only tossed a few pieces of bread, a little boy walks over to the man and they start to talk. The man has stopped tearing off and tossing little pieces of bread. This frustrates the ducks. He has a lot of bread left! He shouldn't be focusing on some stupid conversation! He should be focusing on tearing off and tossing little pieces of bread!

The ducks consider quacking a little—to remind the man that he is in the middle of important bread work—but they don't want to be rude. Because they really do appreciate the bread work he has done so far. It's just really frustrating that his priorities have gotten so out of order.

The man breaks the bread in half and hands one of the halves to the little boy.

And now they're both tearing off and tossing little pieces of bread!

Clean Beak and Beak With Spot are in full agreement: This is paradise.

Though the ducks had planned to leave this place sometime in the afternoon, now they're thinking that it makes absolutely no sense for them to leave this place—this paradise—so soon.

And Beak With Spot is starting to suspect that he was too quick to dismiss that hot water woman's bright light.

Sunk Cost

For at least the last five minutes I've wanted to say something but haven't said anything. It is not very nice, in my view, to risk ruining another person's (possibly) positive experience.

But finally I force myself to lean over and whisper "Do you think this is any good?"

The response, which arrives almost instantly, is "Let's get out of here."

As we exit the movie theater and enter the night I realize that my previous view might have been totally wrong: instead of trying to preserve another person's feelings—which you probably don't even come close to understanding anyway—you should be honest and direct and save everyone involved a lot of time.

Outside the movie theater a big fountain is doing its work.

Some street lamps are lit—softly.

Clouds block the stars—or at least I assume they do: since I can't see any stars I can't actually say, with 100% certainty, that stars are actually up there.

145

We're moving—not in the direction of home—without anything remotely resembling a plan.

Before too long we're standing at the end of the pier. The town is sparkling and the water is black. After a short period of consideration I decide to not jump into the sea. Because, while it could be very refreshing, I don't have a towel.

We go back in the direction we came from. Sometimes words are spoken but, more often, words are not spoken. Either way is fine with me.

Frank Sinatra's voice floats into our ears. It's "Witchcraft" and it's unclear where it's coming from and it's very nice and we don't investigate its origin.

There isn't too much to do around here at this time of night. The café is still open and some people are sitting and eating and talking in the outdoor area, on the sidewalk, but we were already at the café tonight, eating dinner and expressing curiosity about the movie we would soon be watching… So yes, there really isn't anything to do at this point other than go home. Which is fine with me.

Once in a while, over the last few years, we have talked about leaving this town and going to a big city where a lot of things are happening all the time. But I don't know if we will ever actually leave this town. In any case, we're here now and I think we do a pretty good job of making the most of it.

God it felt great to walk out of that movie!

The English Teacher's Dog

Thomas wanted to master the language. Some, including his new employer, would say that he already had. But there were, over the course of each day, several moments in which he wasn't quite sure if his grammar was correct. So, to rectify his situation, he began to take a weekly English lesson.

It wasn't a traditional lesson. He would spend two hours in the living room of a jovial middle-aged man, and they would just talk. About all sorts of things.

About this city, which Thomas found so strange.

About world news, though Thomas always made sure to not say anything that could possibly be considered controversial—which was not difficult, since he didn't really have any views that could be considered, by any reasonable person, controversial.

More than anything else, though, they talked about Thomas's old life, about the family and friends he had left behind when he left his native land. There were sometimes moments, in these parts of their conversations, when Thomas would privately wonder if accepting the job had been the right thing to do. Yes, it was a great opportunity, and it was exactly the kind of work he wanted to be doing… But did that justify the massive upheaval? He couldn't yet say. All he could say was that it wasn't easy, this process of trying to plant himself in this foreign land.

Thomas did not share his doubts with the English teacher. While he enjoyed their conversations, there were certain things he would always keep to himself.

So they would talk, and the English teacher would correct Thomas in the rare moments when he made a grammatical mistake. And whenever Thomas asked a question about the language he would receive a clear and concise answer. He felt like the lessons were helpful.

The best part of the lessons, though, was the dog. The English teacher had a scruffy medium-sized dog that would greet Thomas with great affection upon his arrival. This was exactly the kind of dog Thomas liked. Big dogs, in his view, could be a bit too intimidating. Little dogs usually seemed like they wouldn't be able to survive on their own in the wild, so Thomas considered them needy and, really, pathetic. But a medium-sized dog could take care of himself—without being unnecessarily intimidating—so Thomas considered the medium-sized dog ideal. So he was always pleased to see the English teacher's dog bound over with a swinging tail.

But the dog, despite his energy and fluid movements, certainly wasn't lean. He was chubby.

At least, he was chubby the first few times Thomas saw him…

They had probably completed about one month of lessons when Thomas noticed a change in the dog: it looked like he had lost some weight. But, that day, Thomas did not give the matter much thought. Maybe the English teacher had decided to adjust the dog's diet. Nothing wrong with that. And maybe this would be good for the dog's health.

But, disconcertingly, the dog consistently, from week to week, continued to lose weight.

Though the dog remained as enthusiastic and friendly as ever, Thomas was unsettled.

He considered, more and more frequently, asking the English teacher about the dog. But something kept holding him back. It was the sort of thing, he considered, that maybe just wasn't his business.

Sometimes at work Thomas would suddenly find himself wondering about the dog. Did the dog have a terminal illness? As weeks continued to pass, would the dog keep losing weight until he wasn't much more than a skeleton? With a shake of his head, Thomas would force himself to return his focus to his work; but the English teacher's dog, despite Thomas's efforts, would remain somewhere in the background.

Finally, one afternoon when he and the English teacher were talking about some world news, Thomas blurted out, "Is your dog OK? I'm curious because… Well, it's obvious that he has lost some weight."

"Oh, yes," said the English teacher, somewhat gravely. "My other dog died fairly recently."

"And this dog misses the other dog so much that he no longer has an appetite?"

"Oh, no." The English teacher laughs. "That isn't it at all. You see, my other dog—who was very, very old, by the way—wasn't moving around much in the end and *he* didn't have an appetite. I would try to get him interested in different foods, but he wouldn't eat more than the smallest quantities. So this guy"—the English teacher gestures to the dog, who is lying next to Thomas's chair—"picked up the slack. He ate *everything* the other guy wouldn't. And, in consequence, put on quite a few pounds."

"I see."

"So now this guy eats normal portions. He's almost at his proper weight again."

Looking at the dog now, Thomas realizes that the English teacher is right: the dog is not actually

underweight.　He had simply *seemed* underweight…
because of the memory of his former chubbiness.

Yes, it's clear to Thomas that the English teacher's
dog is not in trouble.

He'll be OK.

Pelicans and Seagull

While wondering about this and that, and why this isn't that, and why that isn't this, the approaching pelicans, together creating a big sky-sailing V, are joined by a seagull, who positions himself in the portside portion of the V—and this aerial development commandeers Alice's mind and jettisons all previous items of thought (i.e., "this" and "that" and various variations of "this" and "that"). Now her entire world is revolving around a single question: how will the pelicans react to the seagull?

Alice does not detect any change in the behavior of the pelicans; they continue to fly in their V formation and do not seem to mind the new presence of the seagull. Together the pelicans and the seagull fly along, now drifting a bit waterward, now propelling themselves a bit skyward, but always maintaining a fairly consistent altitude, and always moving through the air with enviable smoothness, elegant ease, just beyond the edge of the land, over water blue and black and white; and these gravity-defiant creatures seem unbothered by the muscular wind, which pulls long white hair out of waves. Waves that proceed to batter rocks. Rocks that are between what they once were and the dust they will someday be.

Daniel is saying something. Though he is sitting right next to her, on this fine weathered bench, she had almost lost all awareness of his presence. Probably because of that interesting aerial development. So... what is he saying? Oh, something abstract about the future. The future—which in itself is nothing more, and never can be anything more, than an abstraction. But what about that seagull flying in formation with those pelicans? They are almost out of sight. Did Daniel even notice that interesting aerial development? It is the kind of thing—like so many other things—that is all too easy to miss. When one is not paying particularly close attention to one's surroundings.

She notices that he is no longer talking, and she doesn't exactly know what he just said, and she wonders if she should ask him to repeat what he just said.

All too soon, Daniel knows, the sun will go away and darkness will arrive. Darkness is, in a way, a great unifier: so many of the details of different things become imperceptible—at least to the human eye—so it looks like the differences between things have been erased, looks like the many different things on the planet have been transformed—under the stars and the moon or under the stars and no moon or under no stars and a vague moon or under no stars and no moon, depending on local weather and the moon's orbit—into a single big dark chunk of reality. Until the sun returns and articulates, once again, the many beautiful differences.

Daniel wonders where, when the darkness arrives, they will be.

"What do you think we should do," says Daniel, "for dinner?" And then, in response to the unintelligible sound that is Alice's response, he mentions a few of the restaurants they've seen over the course of the week but haven't yet tried. "Since this is our final night I think we should go to one of the nicer places."

This is, indeed, the final night of their vacation. And Alice, somewhat to her surprise, is relieved. Because though she had been looking forward to this vacation for weeks—and has, she tells herself, thoroughly enjoyed this vacation, overall—she feels very ready for it to be over. Because when she is away from work the familiar shape of her life dissolves into formlessness. Every vacation day is daunting because there is no established structure—other than the one determined by the movements of the sun—so she and Daniel must build a structure every vacation day. And their structures sometimes feel pretty rickety. Of course there is a certain enjoyment to be had in deciding exactly what to do each day, in having a lot of control over one's time and activities... But the stress!

With the option to do almost anything at all, how is one to feel as though the choices one is making are the correct choices? How do you convince yourself that what you are doing is not the opposite of what you should be doing? Alice really doesn't know. All of this is overwhelming.

Sitting next to Daniel on this bench by the sea and reflecting on their week here, she actually feels like they did good things during their week here, like they made good use of their week here, like they really had a really good time. But it simultaneously feels all too possible—painfully possible—that they somehow could have made significantly better choices each day. In a different reality she could be sitting on this same bench and reflecting on a significantly better version of this week than the version they just experienced here, in this particular reality.

It will be nice to put all of this behind her and return to work, nice to return to an established structure in which she knows exactly what she should be doing at all times and doesn't have to wonder if there is something better that she should be doing with her time. Because converting a free moment's infinite possibilities into a single decision is exhausting.

Alice still hasn't submitted an intelligible response to Daniel's inquiry about dinner, and he wonders if she has listened to anything he has said since they sat on this bench. Annoyance enters his head, and grows, and grows, and grows—and abruptly disappears, due to his realization that he hasn't actually said anything particularly important. He decides to do his best to appreciate this view. Waves are still battering rocks and birds are still… A seagull is flying with a scoop of pelicans.

"Look at that seagull," says Alice, pointing.

"I was just looking at that seagull," says Daniel. "Trying to be a pelican… It's good to have a dream."

"The pelicans seem to have accepted him. He joined them when they were flying by a few minutes ago, and since he's still with them they must have accepted him."

The pelicans and the seagull—who is now, Alice and Daniel suppose, an honorary pelican—continue to fly along, now drifting a bit waterward, now propelling themselves a bit skyward. All of this is pleasant. Even with the loud sounds of waves wearing down rocks.

"What do you think we should do?"

Daniel proposes dinner at the French restaurant, and Alice thinks that is a very good idea.

Evan Pellervo

The Woods

A moose looks up at the sky.

Clouds move and conceal the sun.

Four people, not too far away from the moose, look up at the sky.

These woods were, due to the high density of trees all around, already fairly dark before the action of the clouds, and now these woods are, naturally, even darker. But a light breeze is still gently conducting the leaves—the product is a comforting, vaguely nostalgic rustle—and birds are still making their chirps and hoots and whistles and trills, so not one of the four people walking, single file, on this narrow, narrow path feels like anything has actually been diminished.

How long have these people been walking? And where are they going?

It's hard to know when and where this all began, and what the purpose—if there even is a purpose—is. Because these woods have the unsettling ability to make one almost forget that anything outside of these woods actually exists. It's hard to know how these woods work... But, for whatever reason, these people in these woods almost feel like they have spent their whole lives walking right here, on this narrow, narrow path.

The moose, still unseen by the people, is watching the people.

The space ahead begins to change. Everything is getting brighter. The density of the trees is decreasing.

The four people emerge from the woods. Ahead, a little slope covered with overgrown grass descends to a little lake. Standing on the other side of the little lake is a little house.

Yes: this was simply a late afternoon walk without any pre-determined purpose other than to get some fresh air.

It was a startlingly good walk, as the woods had helped the people forget—temporarily—their day-to-day concerns. But it is good that they are now almost back at the little house: they are all planning to leave very early in the morning, to return to the city, and should really start packing soon.

The people enter the little house.

The moose moves down the little slope, through the overgrown grass, and reaches the edge of the little lake. The moose lowers his big nose and drinks some cool, clear water.

Clouds move and reveal the sun.

Bloom

The cars on the highway—many moving more slowly than usual because of a three-car accident that is no longer physically obstructing passage (the three not terribly damaged cars were recently moved into the median) but continues to keep things slow because many drivers want to inspect the damage—create two long loose chains of lights in the night, glowing in long graceful curves, one chain composed of various whites and one chain composed of various reds.

If looked at individually and closely, each car's lights may bother your eyes, and each car may seem like a prospective weapon. Sometimes when considering the distractedness—attributable to daily concerns and devices for distant communications—of so many drivers, it seems almost a miracle that more people aren't killed by these propulsive steel objects. Sometimes these propulsive steel objects, along with many of the other trappings of civilization, seem ugly. And sometimes you may even think, at least fleetingly, that too much of the whole "technological progress" thing is simply too removed from nature; but these propulsive steel objects, with their headlights and taillights, were created by us, and since we emerged from nature we are nature, so maybe it isn't too unreasonable to view these propulsive steel objects, with their headlights and taillights, as yet another bloom of the natural world.

Is a fresh steel sheet really so different from a cactus flower?

The headlights and taillights stretching out across the night, floating and glowing, maybe aren't too dissimilar—especially if you take off your glasses or find some other way to evade the oppression of details—to the aurora borealis. Since an aurora can usually only be seen at or somewhat close to the top or bottom of our planet, and only occurs when certain particles participating in a dramatic event on the surface of the sun are abruptly propelled millions and millions of miles across the solar system and happen to get captured by our planet's magnetic field, most people have not seen the aurora borealis or the aurora australis. Most people have, however, seen the seemingly countless lights of cars glowing in the night, floating at various speeds along highways. So while we are in the midst of a sometimes-disagreeable steel bloom, we also create our own beautiful auroras every second of every day.

The Popular Television Program

Though Morton had expected the streets to be quiet, he hadn't expected them to be *this* quiet.

It is 8:04 in the evening, decades ago. The television program everyone has been talking about for weeks began four minutes ago—which was the exact moment when Morton put on his tweed coat in order to feel comfortable outside the massive brutalist structure that contains his apartment, out in the late winter air.

So, yes: this is a moderately busy part of the city, and now the streets are devoid of all life save Morton. Everyone else is inside, watching the television program that is, indisputably, popular.

As an astronomer, Morton is well aware that this is a full moon night; but, sadly, clouds in the sky are concealing the solar system. Oh well.

Walking along, from the light of one streetlamp and into darkness and into the light of another streetlamp and into darkness, etc., he feels like he is the only person on the planet. It is a very peaceful feeling—until a bus trundles by and shatters his reverie.

162

But then the bus is gone, and everything is quiet again, and then snow begins to fall, and the snow makes the world even more quiet.

When he gets back to the apartment he will ask how the television program was even though he doesn't actually care.

Great White Shark

It's New Year's Day. In the past my friend and I have jumped into the bay on New Year's Day. The bay is very cold, but I have never regretted going in. But I am almost never excited about going in, because it really is very cold.

The afternoon is almost over and I haven't heard from my friend. Maybe he's busy with something else. Maybe he forgot about our tradition. That's fine with me. I could reach out to him—there's no reason why I shouldn't—but I don't really want to jump in.

Time to start a new book.

When I've only read three paragraphs, my phone rings. I don't want to answer. I answer.

"Are you ready to jump into the bay?"

No, I think. "Yes," I say.

So we meet and walk to the beach. The day is cold and I know the water is cold.

There are two ways to get into water: fast and slow. My friend and I have always used the former approach, which is why I'm surprised, as I drop my towel onto the sand, to see him standing in the water, motionless, with the water only reaching his ankles.

Trying to not think, I run into the water. It is, as I knew it would be, very cold. But, as I swim as fast as I can, I feel very alive.

When I've swum out a ways I stop and turn around, and see my friend standing in exactly the same place. I make some gestures to indicate that he should get in the water, but he doesn't. Oh well.

I swim farther—and then I see it: the sea otter.

Someone recently told me that a sea otter jumped into her friend's kayak. Apparently the sea otter didn't do anything, just sat there for a while.

But another person told me that a sea otter clawed him once.

This sea otter is eating something. Hard to tell what. But I can tell that his teeth are very sharp.

I swim in the other direction. Then I float.

My friend is sitting on the sand. Other people are on the beach, too, doing various things.

A few streets up the hill, two big trees are catching the sun.

The sun won't be around much longer.

Floating here, a powerful thought arrives: even if a great white shark bites me in half right now, I'll keep living.

House In Rain

This is a room in a house.

Above the ceiling is night sky, and beyond the night sky are stars, and beyond the stars are other things—most of which remain unknown.

The unknown will, at least for now, remain unknown. But this room in this house is, to a certain extent, knowable. Because almost everything in this room is visible and simple.

Three chairs. A table. Nine books. A CD player with fourteen CDs stacked on top of it. A person.

That's pretty much it.

The person puts a CD into the CD player. Sibelius's 5th Symphony awakens.

Within seconds rain begins to fall onto the roof of this house—and, presumably, onto things around the roof of this house; it's hard to say definitively, at least for now, because the rain's contact with the roof is so loud that it's hard to tell if the rain is falling onto anything else.

Time to investigate: the person goes over to the window and looks through the glass. Yes: rain is falling onto the road as well. That makes sense: rain rarely falls onto only one house.

In some moments the sounds of the rain work well with Sibelius.

In some moments the sounds of the rain seem to contradict Sibelius.

The beyond-description symphony ends. Another CD is not put into the CD player. After listening to Sibelius's 5th Symphony, what would be the point of listening to something else?

The rain is still going. The light in this room is turned off. The light in the next room is turned on—an action which effectively turns the next room into this room—and the person gets into bed and opens a book. The rain is still going. Eyes are on the page, but words are not read. Up until now it has been a good book... But how can one focus on a book when one has access to such wonderful rain sounds?

Maybe the rain will continue and continue and continue and eventually lift up this house and carry it away to exotic lands and delightful adventures.

The rain is still going.

Will we reach exotic lands?

Will we partake in delightful adventures?

Well, we can, at least for now, dream.

The book is placed on the nightstand.

The light is turned off and the rain stops immediately.

This house is dark and this person can't hear anything.

This is a moment in which one could easily mistake the world for a tranquil place.

This moment is enough for now.

Pyramid of Hay

Leo has never lived in the country, so he always finds his visits to his grandparents' house interesting. Upon his arrival, he and his parents and his grandparents usually talk for a while: his grandparents comment on how much he has grown since they last saw him; his grandparents ask him what grade he is in now; his parents ask his grandparents a few questions about how things are going with them. And then the conversation is usually over and Leo is pretty much left to his own devices.

The cows are usually Leo's first stop. There are usually ten or so in the pasture in the front of the house, really not doing much at all. Sometimes flies are buzzing around their eyes. Leo has often wondered if the flies bother the cows, or if the cows don't even notice the flies, or if the cows have simply grown to accept the flies— which would probably make sense since, as far as Leo can tell, the cows can't really do anything about the flies anyway.

The creek is usually Leo's second stop. Well, it's called a river, but it fits Leo's definition of a creek. It's around the other side of the house, at the bottom of an overgrown slope, and Leo likes to skip stones across its surface. Aside from ping pong—which he occasionally plays with one of his parents or one of his cousins who lives a few miles away—skipping stones is probably his favorite activity around here.

He really enjoys skipping stones.

Down at the creek today, as he searches for a good flat stone, he remembers being out here last year with one of his cousins, who is several years older and likes to hunt ducks. Earlier on that visit Leo had expressed interest in shooting a duck, since it would definitely be a new experience, so his cousin brought his gun over and they went for a walk along the bank of the creek. To Leo's surprise, they actually found a couple of ducks. After reminding Leo about gun safety, his cousin handed him the gun. Leo got one of the ducks in his sights, held his breath—and couldn't pull the trigger. After telling his cousin that he couldn't shoot the duck, he handed the gun back to his cousin, who shot the duck.

Not long after that Leo felt kind of pathetic: he wasn't a vegetarian, so there really was no good reason, he figured, to not shoot that duck. But even though, today, he still feels kind of pathetic about not shooting that duck, he has absolutely no intention of shooting any ducks in the near future.

There's a little swimming hole not too far away. Reaching down, Leo feels the water with his right hand.

It feels pretty cold.

Forty or so years ago his grandfather built a sauna. Leo hopes he'll get the chance to use it today. They say he's still too young to use it on his own.

His fate is in the hands of others.

Anyhow, now it's time for Leo's usual third stop: the big barn. Which was also built by his grandfather. As he approaches the big barn, he hopes this is the time of year he thinks it is…

And it is! The barn is full of hay!

Well, maybe not *full* of hay, but the vast majority of the interior consists of a pyramid of hay.

Leo begins his journey to the top. Maybe country life will turn out to be the life for him. Sure, it would be a pretty big change from the life he has known so far… But when one has a pyramid of hay to climb, what more does one need?

Leo reaches the summit. He touches the dusty rafters. He breathes deeply.

Hay.

It smells good.

Hay.

It smells wonderful.

Hay.

He'll stay up here for a while.

Some Night Music

Far away, across the river and way to the east and barely seeable, a golden train slides across black hills. She is watching it closely. Recently she was on a train just like it, moving through that exact same sliver of the world, and from that recent train she had seen the far away city lights where she is standing now, but she hadn't been able to see any of the details of her immediate surroundings, of the unilluminated hillside in which the train tracks were embedded. From Seat 21 in Carriage 4, the only thing about her immediate surroundings that had been obvious was that many trees were close to the tracks—again and again and again they interrupted her view of the far away city lights—but what did the trees actually look like? And what kinds of things were going on between the trees? What kinds of life could be found?

It had simply been too dark for answers. Reasonable guesses could have been made—but there is nothing like seeing something with your own eyes.

Now she stands by the river, on which lights of this foreign city are reflected and stretched. When they were walking from the train station to their lodging the sky was cloud-filled and starless, but one minute ago a cloud directly above her head moved a little, allowing a constellation to be seen. She looks up at the constellation, then back at the city lights on the river, and tells herself that this—everything around her—really deserves to be appreciated. *Appreciate this*, she thinks. *Experience gratitude. Right now.*

Annoyingly this does not quite work. Sometimes, despite your best efforts, you can't think your way into an emotion.

Her phone rings.

"I'm sorry," says the voice emerging from the device, "but I'm not going to be able to leave the room. You'll have to eat on your own."

"Should I bring anything back for you? Food? Medicine? Both?"

"Nothing. I'm going to try to throw up again. But you… Have fun. Bye."

She puts her phone away and looks in the direction of the river—but isn't really looking at anything, because she is wondering what she should do. Even though she hasn't eaten anything since the morning, she isn't really hungry. There isn't really anything specific that she wants to do right now; and there are, at least for now, no obligations. It's nice here by the river, and there isn't really any reason why she can't stay here—if she wants—for a long, long, long time.

Not too far away stands a big, nicely lit, somewhat proud-looking bridge, and without even a hint of consideration she begins to walk toward the bridge. When adrift with nowhere to go, you can go anywhere.

In this moment she is as convinced of her freedom as she will ever be.

As she moves parallel to the river people continue to materialize and sounds—including music she can't hear clearly enough to describe—are always changing. Noticing a branch in front of her, lying on cobblestones, she stops. She looks around; no trees are nearby. How did this branch end up here? There must be a story. A story that will never be known by her. If she really tried she could find out, somehow, what kind of tree this branch came from—*but what would be*, she wonders, *the point? A thing is whatever it happens to be, and whatever you decide to call it really doesn't matter. Not only does the kind of tree this branch came from not matter, but even going to the trouble of calling this branch a branch seems stupid; this branch should, like everything else, simply be thought of as yet another fragment of reality.*

She kicks the fragment of reality into the river, saying "And on to your next adventure!"—and continues her own adventure, this night stroll in this foreign city.

As the music crystallizes her interest increases. Eventually she finds herself in a crowd, looking at a makeshift stage on the edge of the river. Eleven musicians are playing with precision and smiles. All of the instruments are acoustic, which she thinks is too unusual these days. There are two mandolins, two guitars, a viola, a bass, three string instruments she can't identify with certainty, a tambourine, and a flute. Most of the players also sing—in the language of this country, unsurprisingly, which she only partly understands. But the absence of complete comprehension actually makes the music more engaging: absence creates room for imagination.

The first song she listens to with total focus is triumphant, as though big challenges have been surmounted, and now we can enjoy ourselves.

The second song is full of nostalgia—but, though reviewing memories of long-ago good things can be painful, at least we have the memories. Of whatever has been, in whatever way, lost.

The third song is the hardest one to grasp. On one hand it seems to be about fortitude in the face of great adversity, about the drive to press on, to do what must be done to get somewhere—where?—but, on the other hand, an unmistakable indifference is present. A certain disregard for... It's like there's an awareness of the arbitrariness and ultimate insignificance of the goal—but

one will, nevertheless, continue to work toward the goal…
And if it doesn't work out, who cares?

This is a phenomenal performance. As a person who has not only played guitar for years, but who in college studied classical guitar while mainly studying economics, she knows good musicianship when she hears it, and this is, undeniably, good musicianship. As far as she can tell, this band has no weak member. Everyone is doing excellent and crucial work—and doing so, refreshingly, without even a trace of gravity. There is obvious joy.

This could actually be the best concert she has ever experienced. Because it's even more than their wonderful playing and singing: it's being surrounded by people who seem happy; it's that shining river rolling along; it's that proud bridge gracefully hopping over a boat; it's the warm lights of the city dancing all around; it's the constellations twinkling; it's the promise of life.

This could be as good as it gets.

This—well, *that*, what's going on up there on the stage—should be her life. For years the majority of her time has been devoted to numbers; yes, they are often important numbers that describe and predict aspects of reality, but from her new perspective those numbers seem way too abstract, way too removed from the happenings of the immediate world around her body. From where she is existing. She suddenly can't quite believe she has, for so long, been essentially addicted to numbers, and to screens and pieces of paper that contain them. Is that really how she should spend her life?

She decides she will try to join this wonderful band. Of course communication could be a bit of a challenge—listening to their singing has made clear how little of this language she actually understands—and of course it's possible that, even though she feels certain she's a good enough guitarist to be a good addition, they may simply not want her. So… But, in any case, no matter what happens with this particular band, she will find *some* way, she informs herself, to make music the central part of her life.

Wait—what? You are going, she thinks, *to change your whole life because you happen to like this music? That is just… insane.*

She listens to and thoroughly enjoys the rest of the performance, then pleasantly wanders around the city for a while, then eats a snack—she still isn't really hungry, but feels like she should eat at least something—then makes her way back to their lodging.

She opens the door and crosses the threshold and closes the door.

"How was it out there?"

She considers mentioning that she heard what was probably the best concert of her life. "Fine. I basically just wandered around aimlessly. Which was pleasant. But you didn't really miss anything."

About a mile away the branch she kicked into the river spins slowly under stars, accompanied by a hospitable current and a friendly wind.

Nautical Charts

It's three in the afternoon and The Admiral still hasn't eaten any lunch because he has been so focused on his nautical charts. Though there is no longer any practical reason for him to review his nautical charts—he is well into retirement, his seafaring days are far, far behind him—he still finds himself spending quite a bit of time with his nautical charts every day.

They remind him of all the things he did.

They remind him of all the places he saw.

They make him feel proud and nostalgic.

That sure was a fine career! He'd had real purpose back then!

Though The Admiral sometimes suspects that he spends too much time reminiscing, too much time living in the past, he hasn't identified a better way to spend his time. But if he *could* manage, somehow, to feel alive—and useful—in the present again… Well, that would be nice.

But at least he has his nautical charts.

A thud interrupts The Admiral's progress across the Indian Ocean. His head immediately turns toward the sound, toward the window—and nothing looks unusual. The Admiral walks over to the window, opens the window, sticks his head out of the room, and looks down. A small bird is lying on the ground. The bird appears to be lying quite unnaturally, but it's hard to tell because this is the second floor and The Admiral's vision isn't what it used to be.

Less than a minute later The Admiral is outside, crouching next to the bird. One wing is bent very oddly and the head is bent very oddly and feathers are ruffled. Though the heart is still going, its beat seems irregular.

The Admiral sighs sadly, feeling certain that the bird is in the process of dying.

The Admiral feels certain that he should kill the bird right away, since death seems like the only way the bird's suffering will ever be alleviated. And, if The Admiral *doesn't* do anything, who knows how long the bird will remain here in agony before finally dying?

But even though The Admiral firmly believes that killing the bird is the compassionate thing to do... Well, for whatever reason, he just can't seem to do it. Which makes him feel like a complete coward. He spent his whole career doing challenging work that had significant consequences, and now he can't even manage to kill—to help!—a small bird.

Turning around to return to his study, The Admiral feels worthless.

The Admiral tries to re-immerse himself in his nautical charts, in the Indian Ocean—and fails miserably.

Walking over to the still-open window, he sticks his head out of the room and looks down. The bird appears unchanged.

The Admiral tries to re-immerse himself in his nautical charts, in the Atlantic Ocean this time—and fails miserably.

Walking over to the still-open window, he sticks his head out of the room and looks down. The bird appears to be…

Less than thirty seconds later The Admiral is outside, approaching the bird, and… Yes! The bird *is* standing! Some feathers are still ruffled, but everything else about the bird seems OK. The Admiral isn't certain, though, since his vision isn't what it used to be, so he keeps approaching…

The bird flies away, and The Admiral suddenly feels very optimistic about the future.

As he prepares a snack in the kitchen he decides to stay away from his nautical charts for a while.

Mediterranean Cypresses

The function has been over for hours. The inn is quiet because most of the people inside the inn are asleep. Outside the inn a sleeping dog sneezes, wakes up, and begins to walk around on the gravel. The jagged sounds made by paws on gravel reach the ears of a pajamaed boy inside the inn, lying on a cot, wide awake.

Leo gets off the cot—realizing, as he does, that he has wanted to do so for a long time—and moves to the window. The moon, which was full yesterday, makes it easy to see the dog, who moves with his nose close to the gravel, as though sniffing for something specific. Is he searching for something?

Beyond the dog some Mediterranean cypresses are using the moonlight to create shadows.

Beyond the Mediterranean cypresses a river is a silver thread. Thread a needle with the river and sew the river into the sky for something completely different.

Beyond the river some hills are preparing to conceal the moon.

Leo opens the window and the air in the room changes and the jagged gravel sounds sound louder—and

183

now he can also hear bugs hum. This could be considered a concert.

Standing there, he stops listening to the concert and stops paying attention to the view and thinks about the day. He supposes there is nothing *actually* wrong with how the day went... What's frustrating is that even though he'd interacted with many different people over the course of the day, in every interaction there was a noticeable distance. All of the adults he talked with seemed to say the same kinds of things, perfunctorily asked the same generic questions, and didn't supply any interesting answers to any of his much more interesting questions. He really wants to learn about how different adults live their different lives. And there is something else, too. So often he has wondered... Is there a Great Secret? Something important about life that he ought to know by now but, for whatever reason, does not?

Though he had hoped to obtain at least *some* fascinating and valuable information at his aunt's wedding, he did not manage—and it is so annoying!—to obtain even satisfactory information. Nothing had been illuminated today. The big problem, Leo theorizes, was that the adults simply didn't want to authentically engage with a non-adult. Which Leo finds extremely frustrating since, having accumulated twelve full years of life, he views himself as essentially an adult. After all, he knows that those trees out there are called Mediterranean cypresses—and how many of the adults at the wedding knew that? It's possible, he supposes, that they all knew that—but he doubts it. A few other kids were in attendance, and Leo supposes he could have engaged with them—but they were all at least two years younger than him, so he feels fairly certain that he couldn't possibly have learned anything worthwhile from them.

Looking across the little sitting room, he sees that the door to the bedroom is still closed. His hand goes through the space between the window and the windowsill and feels the night air. After a glance at his cot—which is actually quite comfortable—he moves, quietly, to the exit and, quietly, exits.

When he steps onto gravel the dog turns around to see who's there. Leo walks toward the dog and the dog turns around and trots away, moving beyond some of the Mediterranean cypresses, into a more distant part of the night. Leo stops walking and looks down at the gravel. In this moonlight each little stone is so sharply defined that he suddenly feels like his previous walks on this gravel were conducted in a deep haze of obliviousness, as he hadn't had even the slightest awareness of the incorrigible individuality of each of these little stones

Why he is out here? The dog is probably why he had come out here. But now the dog is gone and, as far as Leo can tell, there really isn't anything to do out here. There are a few things to look at, but none of it is particularly exciting. With the moon communicating so much light he could probably make it to the river OK… But actually maybe not, since the moon is now touching one of the hills and probably won't be helpful for much longer.

So it looks like this is it. No adventure here. Leo remembers the pirates he was reading about in "Treasure Island" this morning. What an incredible time Jim Hawkins has! It's sad, but Leo really believes that if someone were to write a story about him, about his life right now, it definitely would not be a story that he would want to read. Simply too boring. Not nearly enough action. Because what is he, Leo, doing with his life? He is standing on some gravel. Around him are hills, the moon, some Mediterranean cypresses, a sleep-filled inn. Somewhere nearby there's a dog. That's it. Oh, there's also the river, not too far away. But *that's* it. Nothing exciting is happening here.

Yes, nothing exciting is happening here… But at least nothing *bad* is happening here. And at least this air isn't too cold.

Suddenly Leo feels convinced that if there is a Great Secret, the adults don't know what it is either.

It actually kind of seems like these mysterious Mediterranean cypresses know something. But any knowledge they have is, in all likelihood, undeliverable.

The dog, now lying on land no longer illuminated by the moon, watches Leo, and Leo watches some little stones and listens, once again, to the concert of the bugs.

Over Before You Know It

This is, for me, a foreign land.

The two of us are sitting under a big tree under a sky made of many colors. Other adults are drinking and smoking outside the bar over there and children are playing soccer in this little park and bodies in the little church graveyard on the other side of this little park are being, slowly, consumed.

Sometimes I wonder—before telling myself to stop wondering and pay attention to what is actually happening—how I ended up here, with this particular person. An incomprehensible number of minuscule and massive things happened in exactly the right order to allow this connection to exist.

Shadows are very long and everything that is in the sun's light is kind of golden. Some blades of grass close to us, screaming with life, look like they might explode with light. Very soon the horizon will consume the sun, and the contrasts between things will be reduced. Things will appear more similar and more prosaic, but they will actually still be as unique and as good as they are right now, during this sunset.

Our conversation is wonderful. A transcript could be provided, but what is more important than what is said is the *way* what is said is said; and though I could provide some description of the way we're talking, it probably wouldn't feel accurate enough—meaningful enough?—so I'm not going to do that. I don't want to get it wrong.

Or maybe I just don't want to reveal anything too personal.

You'll have to use your own imagination.

Or not.

Anyhow, very soon we will be moving in different directions. And I'll just say, before leaving, that an unexpected and unsustainable connection with someone is like a striking sunset: it's very nice and it's over far too soon, but at least you were there to see it.

Mai Tai In The Seventh

"I'll tell you what you want," he says. "Mai Tai. Running in the seventh race. The return won't be tremendous, but you'll be happy. Trust me. Mai Tai in the seventh. To win."

And then he's gone and she's alone with the statue of Seabiscuit and two swaying palm trees and a fluttering American flag. Well, she isn't *actually* alone, there are quite a few other people around—some are hurrying with a clear destination in mind, some are ambling along with apparent aimlessness, some are discussing horses and jockeys with gravity, some are laughing, some are standing still and not making a sound and staring at their racing forms—but she is barely aware of their existence. For her, all of life has been compressed into one question: *How do I win?*

She doesn't know that guy well, but she kind of knows him; a few months ago he gave her a tip that worked. That one turned out to be a hell of a horse. But that was then and this is now, and she only just got here and hasn't yet reviewed today's racing form for herself—

which, as a meticulous bettor who hates to leave anything to chance, she must do.

Moving toward the grandstand, she begins to observe the people who happen to be in her field of vision. The variety is incredible; so many different kinds of lives are lived. And today they all ended up here, and she senses that none of them would prefer to be anywhere else on the planet. This whole place is infused with anticipation, with an eagerness about a future that feels likely and close: wallets will soon be heavier.

As she walks she lightly hits her left shoulder with her racing form, which she rolled up tightly, into a tube, without really noticing what she was doing. A shaggy dog sneezes and she remembers Lucky. What a fine dog he was! Time and memory are so strange. Lucky died over ten years ago, and for at least a year she thought about him multiple times a day—but then his absence underwent the transformation that everything undergoes upon establishing consistency: it became normal. When did she last think about Lucky?

Though she really tries, she is unable to remember when she last remembered.

The grandstand is not too crowded and she quickly finds a nice place to sit. The racetrack is pretty much empty and the mountains beyond the racetrack are pretty much empty. It's good that those mountains are there, for their monumentality reflects the monumentality of what goes on at this racetrack: this is a place of grand transfigurations: this is where some dreams become reality and where some dreams become nothing.

It hasn't been cloudy like this in a long, long, long time, and rain actually seems possible. She has always loved how rain heightens the drama of a race. Hooves sink deeper into the surface; fresh mud flies out in all directions; jockeys' colorful silks get splattered, filthy; it's all so beautiful.

In her mind the possibility of rain is an extremely good sign: at this point rain would be different and special in almost exactly the same way a successful day at the racetrack would be different and special: if the weather changes, her luck will change. For so long nothing—at the racetrack or anywhere else—has gone her way. Her life seems to be moving toward only one thing: destitution. Which is why it's so important for her to win big today. Which is why it's time for her to unroll her racing form, open it up, and get serious.

She crosses her legs and puts the racing form on her left knee and leans forward. *If you work properly now*, she tells herself, *you will fix your trajectory.*

So. Let's see… Mai Tai in the seventh…

There it is! Right in front of her! Exactly what she has been waiting for has finally arrived—and with such clarity! She has found the horse that will gallop her into a better future—and it sure as hell isn't Mai Tai. It's one of the horses running against Mai Tai, and his name is Remember Lucky.

Remember Lucky! That's what she was *just* doing, only a few minutes ago and for the first time in longer than she can remember. This can't be just a coincidence. No, this is much more: this is spooky action at a distance.

Several times she has found herself reviewing books on quantum entanglement in the library. It's a bizarre phenomenon that has been demonstrated with electrons and tiny metal drums, and it could be, she senses, a key to unlock the universe and look inside. To see deeper relationships and finally understand how this big cosmic machine really works. Spooky action at a distance is when the condition of one thing is connected with and affected by the condition of another thing, even if the two things are separated by a lot of space. Some physicists say this connection can exist across billions of miles.

Though there are many aspects of entanglement that still elude comprehension, it seems pretty obvious to her that there are many more connections between seemingly separate parts of the universe—of existence—than one can see in everyday life or articulate through regular logic. "There are more things in heaven and earth, Horatio, than are dreamt of in your philosophy," said Hamlet—and she agrees with him: she just *knows* something strange is going on here. And she also knows she'll probably never know what exact particles and forces she is entangled with.

But it seems pretty obvious to her that the universe triggered the memory of Lucky to let her know that she should bet on Remember Lucky. Of course this situation would be very different if she still remembered Lucky all the time; but since this was the first time she'd remembered Lucky in a long, long, long time, the message is clear.

What's especially great about how all of this has turned out is that Remember Lucky is a long shot. Today she will make what is, for her, a fortune—because she is now on her way to take all of her remaining dollars out of her bank account.

She is smiling. She is so grateful: this kind of gift is incredibly rare. And she's proud of herself for not blindly following that guy's Mai Tai tip, but for figuring things out for herself.

About one hour later she is approaching the betting window, and she feels totally ready to put everything on Remember Lucky. Of course she knows it's possible that, despite having so much science on her side, the seventh race will not go her way and Remember

Lucky will lose. But she really doubts it. In the very near future she'll have her big win and her life will change, she really believes it. And if she is wrong and loses all her money, her life will still change, just in a different direction—and change is good. Life is too short for this much of the same thing. As she waits in the short line to place her bet, she thinks, again and again and again, *This is the day your life will change. This is the day your life will change.*

And now, with a fresh and full-of-potential ticket in her hand, that is a certainty.

When she gets to the edge of the racetrack rain begins to fall and she likes how it touches her skin and how it makes this place smell and she sees horses in the distance and she looks again at those monumental mountains and it seems like everything is perfectly connected and she feels like her body might explode with hope—and she wouldn't trade the feeling for anything in the world.

A second volume
of Short Happy Stories
is underway.

Milton Keynes UK
Ingram Content Group UK Ltd.
UKHW010732220224
438165UK00001B/2

9 798989 578702